BUT YOU
SCARED ME
THE MOST

BUT YOU SCARED ME THE MOST

AND OTHER SHORT STORIES

JOHN MANDERINO

ACADEMY
CHICAGO

Copyright © 2016 by John Manderino
All rights reserved
Published by Academy Chicago Publishers
An imprint of Chicago Review Press Incorporated
814 North Franklin Street
Chicago, Illinois 60610
ISBN 978-1-61373-475-9

Library of Congress Cataloging-in-Publication Data
Names: Manderino, John.
Title: But you scared me the most : and other short stories /
John Manderino.
Description: First edition. | Chicago, Illinois :
Academy Chicago Publishers, [2016]
Identifiers: LCCN 2015033052 | ISBN 9781613734759
(softcover: acid-free paper)
Classification: LCC PS3563.A46387 A6 2016 |
DDC 813/.54—dc23
LC record available at http://lccn.loc.gov/2015033052

Cover design: John Yates
Interior layout: Nord Compo

Printed in the United States of America
5 4 3 2 1

To Marie

I saw a vampire,
I saw a ghost,
Everybody scared me,
But you scared me the most.

—Randy Newman,
"Last Night I Had a Dream"

CONTENTS

Too Old to Trick-or-Treat, Too Young to Die

When I was eleven I wanted to be a bum, for Halloween I mean. Eleven was a little old for trick-or-treating, I realized, but I was quite small for my age, so it wouldn't look *too* bad, and I wanted the candy.

No, that's not true.

I wish to be honest here.

I wanted to go as a hobo, like all the years before—with burnt cork smeared on my face for a beard, a broken derby hat, a shredded shirt, patches pinned to my pants, a red bandanna full of crumpled paper at the end of a stick over my shoulder, chomping on a stubby rubber cigar—so when people, especially big, round mothers, opened their doors and saw me they would tilt their heads and say "*Awwww*" and want to give me a great big hug, and some even would.

But my mother insisted I go out there this year as someone more "dynamic"—her word—than a derelict asking for a handout. Here's what she had me wear:

1

white shirt, white bow tie, white vest, black pants, and this long black silky cape with a shiny red lining and high, pointy collar. As she straightened it on my shoulders she told me Dracula was actually a very sophisticated person, very self-assured, a *count* after all, who fully owned his own castle.

I'd seen the old Bela Lugosi movie and his castle didn't look very appealing: cobwebs, shadows, and rats.

"An *accomplished* man, Kevin," she added. She herself was an accomplished advertising executive and bridge player, who looked like Lauren Bacall. "Close your eyes," she told me, and began applying eyeliner with a little pencil from her black-beaded purse.

My dad stood nearby in his tweed jacket with elbow patches, puffing on his pipe, reading glasses on his forehead, informing me that Dracula was the eponymous character from the 1897 novel by Irish-born writer Bram Stoker. "One of the most fascinating fictional creations of all time, Kevin." Dad taught high school English. The kids gave him a horrible time, but at home in the evenings he sucked on his pipe and thought of himself as a professor.

As Mom started darkening my eyebrows, Dad assured me that the model for Dracula was a powerful medieval ruler known as Vlad the Impaler. "What about fangs?" he asked my mom.

"Those are for children," she said. "Now, I'm going to put a little bit of this on," she told me, showing me the tube of lipstick. "So don't fuss."

"Oh, I'm not so sure he wants to be wearing lipstick—do you, Kev?"

"Please keep your mouth very still," she said.

"Whom are you addressing?" he asked her.

"You're going to look very striking," she promised me.

"By the way," Dad added, "he was called Vlad the Impaler because of the manner in which he customarily—"

"*There*," she said, stepping back from her canvas. "Go look at yourself in the bathroom."

Dad called out after me, "Don't be alarmed if there's no reflection—I'm kidding, of course."

He meant about vampires and mirrors.

I stood in front of the mirror above the sink. There was definitely a reflection. I nodded in approval at it. Spreading open the cape, I tilted my head back and bared my teeth. Then I dropped my arms, turned around, took a step, whirled, and faced the mirror again. Slowly I spread the cape, slowly smiling.

"Kevin?" my mother called. "Let's go. Time to get out there."

When I came back she handed me a black waxy shopping bag with handles, telling me to keep in mind: "You're not some cute little hobo asking for charity. You're Count Dracula. *Demand* a piece of candy: trick or treat. In other words—"

"An ultimatum," Dad explained.

"Look them deep in the eye," Mom told me, hands on my shoulders, looking me deep in the eye.

"Actually," Dad pointed out, "the phrase *ought* to be 'Treat or trick,' the idea being—"

She turned to him. "Will. You. *Cease?*"

———

It was a warm evening. I walked the dark, tree-lined side streets: alone, alone. I even tossed away the shopping bag. It wasn't candy I wanted. I didn't know *what* I wanted.

Something.

Whenever I saw other trick-or-treaters coming I would hide behind the nearest tree until they passed, because I knew what they would see: some creepy kid too old for Halloween, wearing lipstick.

But as I hid, pressing my back against the hard bark of the tree, with my face turned away, I began feeling more and more secretive, nocturnal, furtive—more and more, that is, like *him*.

Wanting to try myself out on someone, I went up to a house and rang the doorbell. An overweight woman in a dime-store witch's costume opened the door, holding a plastic jack-o'-lantern full of candy. I spread the cape, tilted back my head, and opened my mouth, wide. "Oh *no*," she cried, "it's Dracula! Help, help!" Then she smiled and held out a miniature Tootsie Roll. "Here you are, dear. Where's your bag?"

Shielding my eyes with my caped arm, I backed away from the Tootsie Roll as if from a crucifix, then turned and ran off.

"Don't you want your candy?"

I was running home. I felt ridiculous and ashamed and wanted to get out of this silly costume and into the shower as quickly as I could.

But two guys I recognized from school—eighth graders—were coming up the sidewalk, and I slipped behind a tree.

One of them saw me.

"Check it out," he said, coming over. "It's fuckin' Dracula!"

The taller one joined him and told me I suck. "Get it? You suck?"

"Whoa," the other one said, "is that *lipstick* you're wearing?"

"What're you, a fuckin' queer?"

"Suck on *this*, homo," the shorter one told me, punching me in the stomach, not that hard, but I went down moaning and holding the place with both hands so he wouldn't feel the need to hit me again.

They stood over me:

"Fuckin' faggot."

"Fuckin' fairy."

"Fuckin' fruit."

"Fuckin' freak."

They finally ran out of things to call me that began with the letter F, and went away.

I sat there. It was quiet, just the wind through the dry leaves overhead, whispering horrible secrets, and in the distance two dogs serenading one another across the darkness. *Listen to them*, I thought in a Transylvanian accent, *the children of the night. What music they make!*

I stood up. I rose. I spread my cape. I ran after those bullies, holding out the cape like rippling wings, keeping to lawns so they wouldn't hear my approaching footsteps. When I got close I hid behind a tree, catching my breath, and watched them enter a vacant lot.

Perfect.

I sucked a lungful of air, raced up behind them, and leaped on the smaller one's back, my legs around his waist, arms around his neck. "*Fuck*," he hollered, and carried me a few staggering steps before falling forward into the weeds. I held on. He managed to flip himself over, still under me but facing me now, and I quickly pressed my wide-open mouth to the salty skin of his neck, bit down hard as I could, and broke through, blood coming warm and sweet, and as he laid there—stunned, I suppose—I could feel his heart beating with mine:

Thump-thump, thump-thump, thump-thump . . .

Then his buddy was kicking me in the ribs and I rolled off, onto my back, and didn't care what they did to me.

Afterwards, I managed to stand up and make my way home. My ribs ached, one eye was already closing up, my balls were throbbing, both ears ringing loud, and there was blood in my mouth.

His and mine.

I told my parents a gang of trick-or-treating hobos mugged me and stole my bag. Then I held up my hand to indicate I wasn't taking questions and went to my room. I laid on my back in the dark, a wooden stake embedded in my heart:

Oh God . . . oh fuck . . . oh love . . .

———

I wanted to see him, just see him.

So after school was finally out the following day, I waited by the buses, once again behind a tree. I spotted him. He was with some others, laughing and carrying on—with a large Band-Aid on his neck! That thrilled me so deeply I followed him to his bus. Keeping my face averted—he might have recognized the shiner he gave me—I went and sat in the very back. I wanted to see where he got off, to see where he lived. I watched him sitting there yakking and laughing away with his pals.

Which hurt. Clearly I was the furthest thing from his mind.

He got off alone. I watched out the back window to see which house he walked towards. By the time the bus turned the corner he was heading up the walkway of a two-story brick house with a fake deer on the lawn.

I faced front again, excited by an idea.

———————

That night after dark I slipped out, in my cape, and walked all the way there. I stood along the side of the house, next to a large bush. There was a lighted window on the upper floor. From this angle all I could see was pale blue ceiling, but somehow I was certain, absolutely certain, that this was his room and that he was there, lying on his bed reading a comic book. I spread my cape and stared up at the window, concentrating with all my might:

Come to me.

I pictured him looking up from the page . . .

Come to me.

Pictured him getting up slowly . . .

Come to me.

Crossing the room in a trance . . .

Come to me.

Up to the window . . .

Come to me.
To the window . . .
Come! To! Meee!
I dropped my arms and hung my head.

———————

Mom was still at her bridge club when I got back, Dad in his office grading papers, classical music playing. Standing at attention in front of the mirror above the bathroom sink, still wearing my cape, I watched myself place into my mouth and swallow down, one after the other, all seventeen remaining Tylenols in the bottle. Then I went to my room and laid there in the dark, arms crossed on my chest.

But I started feeling sick. It grew worse. I hurried back to the bathroom and knelt over the toilet, embracing it. When I was through I wiped my mouth with a corner of the cape and sat back on my heels:

If only I could have remained a cute little hobo.

Nevertheless I was glad I wasn't dead, glad to still be around, I honestly was. I got up and threw some water on my face. Then I happened to look in the mirror. Imagine, if you can, my amazement when all I saw was the other side of the bathroom.

I moved to the left, to the right, but I still wasn't there.

Back from her bridge club, my mother came to the door and tried it, then knocked. "Kevin? Are you in there?"

Staring into the empty mirror I touched myself all over. "I'm not . . . sure."

She asked me what in God's name *that* was supposed to mean.

I kept silently begging the mirror: *Please?*

She knocked, rapid and hard, "Kevin, answer me."

My father joined her out there. "Say something to reassure your mother and me, son. The statement *itself* needn't be reassuring but simply the fact that—"

"Damn it, Kevin, *answer!*"

I said, "Mother . . . Father . . . I have good news and bad."

My mother asked for the bad news first.

"I seem . . . to have turned into . . . a vampire."

They were quiet for a moment. Then my father said, "And the good news, son?"

I flung open the cape and threw back my head. "I'm a vampire!"

A Certain Fellow
Named Phil

It's over. I killed her. I'm not sorry. There was no other way.

Her name was Veronica. I called her Ronnie. Ever hear that old song? How's it go? *I'm gonna buy a paper doll that I can call my own.* Well, what if instead of a pitiful little *paper* doll we're talking life-sized, with amazingly realistic skin, beautiful blue eyes, the lids a bit lowered—bedroom eyes—the mouth pronouncing *Oh.* As in, "Oh yes, oh yes, oh yes!"

Ronnie's turn-offs: mean people, TV commercials, pointy objects. Turn-*ons*? The Tijuana Brass, long rainy afternoons, a certain fellow named Phil.

I'm that certain fellow. I'm Phil.

But you know what the really great thing about Ronnie was? In addition to being a wonderfully accommodating sexual partner, she was an extremely good listener. I told her everything, my hopes, my dreams:

"Someday, Ronnie, I would like to invent something."

"Oh, Phil, yes! Oh yes!"

"Something that would benefit all mankind."

"Oh, Phil, when you talk like this, it turns . . . me . . . on!"

"Does it, Ronnie?"

"Oh yes!"

And yet, I must confess, in spite of Ronnie's many wonderful qualities, I often found myself wondering what it might be like to have an *actual* woman instead of a merely inflated one. But here's something interesting. Do you know a woman who's even more inflated than Ronnie *ever* was? Barbara Larson, in Payroll. And she's not even all that attractive. Ronnie put her to shame. Nevertheless I went ahead and asked her out and she agreed, so I took her to a movie, afterwards dinner, paid for everything, had what I *thought* was a very successful evening, at one point even making her laugh a little. Three days later I call her up and ask her out again. She's very sorry.

I said, "Didn't you have a nice time, Barbara?"

"I have to go now."

"I thought we had a *very* nice time."

"*Byyye.*"

Couple days later I call and ask her if she'd like to have a *really* good time and go bowling. She tells me to please leave her alone. So tonight I call and ask her again if she'd care to go bowling. She tells me if I don't leave her alone she's going to inform the police. That was the word she used, "inform."

I took Ronnie back out from under the bed. She was *very* glad to see me, if you know what I mean.

Afterwards we got to talking, like we do. I ended up telling her about Barbara. Big mistake. Ronnie was furious. She called me an asshole and did it ever occur to me that *she* might like to go bowling once in a while?

I told her I was pretty certain that wasn't actually possible.

"Oh, I'm real enough to have sex but not to go bowling, is that what you're saying? I'm just something to stick your dick into?"

"*And* talk to. We talk a lot, Ronnie."

"No, Phil. Not really."

"We're talking *now*, aren't we?"

"No, Phil. Not really."

"How can you say that?"

"I can't. That's the point. You're the only one talking. In fact, this is you talking right now, saying these very words."

Ronnie would sometimes do that when she was upset, throw it in my face about her not being real. But tonight she got downright cruel. Said she wasn't surprised this Barbara woman didn't want to go out with me again.

"Don't," I told her. "You're just upset."

But she wouldn't stop. "I know I act fascinated when you talk to me, my mouth open like 'Oh, how fascinating!' But do you know the real reason my mouth is open like that?"

"Don't, Ronnie."

"Because I'm *yawning*, that's why. Because I'm bored, Phil. Because you are so . . . incredibly . . . boring!"

I grabbed her long, scrawny throat and brought my hands together, and *now* her mouth was open like that because she was trying to breathe.

"Die, bitch, die . . ."

Then, all of a sudden, I saw myself.

I got up and hurried out to the kitchen and stood there naked in the dark. "My God," I thought, "what have I become? What . . . have I . . . become?"

I hung my head and wept, just wept.

Afterwards I felt better, as though I'd woken up from a horrible dream. I headed straight back to the bedroom and stood there in the doorway:

"Ronnie, I am so sorry. I am so ashamed. Please forgive me, honey? Can you?"

She didn't say anything.

"Honey, please? Don't make me beg."

Still no response.

I stepped over to the bed.

"Oh dear God," I whispered.

She had turned old and wrinkled. I checked the sole of her left foot: the cap on the valve was still secure. I must have punctured her somewhere during our struggle. I watched her growing older and older, her mouth *now* open in horror at what was happening to her.

"Goodbye, my love," I told her. "Please try to understand: I couldn't let you talk to me like that. How could I let you get away with talking to me like that?"

She was finally altogether flat, those big lovely breasts having collapsed in on themselves. I rolled her up, took her to the kitchen, wedged her into the garbage can, and closed the lid.

That, I have to say, felt pretty good. Pretty wonderful, in fact.

Now: I'm going to call Barbara Larson one more time. I'm going to give her one more chance. And if she says no again? I'm going to tell her what happened to Ronnie. I'm going to explain to her: that's what happens to *all* inflated women I come across, where they all end up.

See if maybe *that* gets her interested in bowling.

Nessie

There was a song on the radio that fall called "Puff the Magic Dragon," which Joan could hardly stand listening to, it was so heartbreaking. Her older sister Sandra had a pink radio on the shelf above her bed, near Joan's, and whenever "Puff" came on, if Sandra wasn't there, Joan would lie gazing up at the ceiling, and at the part where Jackie Paper came no more and Puff's green scales fell like rain, Joan's *tears* would fall like rain.

Then one morning in her seventh grade geography class Mrs. Costello told them about her trip last summer to Scotland, showing them on the globe: across the Atlantic Ocean, right up there on top of England. They learned a little of its history, that the city of Edinburgh is its capital, about the country's natural resources, and other not very interesting things. But then Mrs. Costello told them about visiting a lake called Loch Ness, "loch" being Scottish for "lake," and about a huge creature that many people believed was living in the lake, called the Loch Ness Monster. Mrs. Costello said, "Yes, Thomas?"

"How could a whole monster live in a lake and people not even be sure?"

"That's a very good question, and I wonder if anyone can answer it—Peter? Is that your hand up?"

"Just scratching, Mrs. Costello."

"Brian? Are you just scratching, too?"

"Because the lake is very big?"

"Exactly. The lake is very, *very* big. Francine?"

"What does it look like?"

"The monster? Well, based on a photograph, which may or may not be authentic, here is what the creature *might* look like," and with remarkable speed she drew something on the board that looked almost exactly the way Joan pictured Puff.

"Yes, Joan?"

"Does he have scales?"

"Very possibly," said Mrs. Costello, and drew some *V*s along the body. "People in the area, by the way, call the creature 'Nessie,'" she said, and wrote that on the board above her drawing.

Joan liked that name for him better than "Loch Ness Monster." Much friendlier sounding.

In English class, which followed geography, Mrs. Costello said that since she had described her trip to Scotland for them, perhaps they should describe for her, in their most legible handwriting, something interesting *they* did over summer break.

They had forty-two minutes.

Joan described for Mrs. Costello her family's trip to—of all places—*Scotland*, visiting the lake where the

Loch Ness Monster lived, and about her falling out of their sailboat and sinking down, down, down, but being rescued by, of all things, the Loch Ness Monster, who took her to his underwater cave where she was finally able to breathe after holding her breath for so long she thought she would burst, and they talked— he could talk, she was so surprised—and he told her how sad he was because people called him a monster but he *wasn't* a monster, he was just big, that's all, and then he started crying, but she hugged his neck and called him "Nessie," and *now* he was crying because of how *happy* he was. But then it was time to head back, her parents would be starting to worry, and she rode toward the shore on his back, which he kept just below the water so you could only see *her*, with her arms out, like she was motorized, and dropped her off near the shallow water, then swam away, back to his cave, while Joan swam the rest of the way to shore. Then everyone gathered around. "What happened?" they all said. But she wouldn't tell them. She knew they would never believe her. And that was by far the most interesting thing that happened all summer, the rest of the summer being mostly boring.

———

"Sandra?" she said.

"What."

"Have you ever heard of Nessie?" Joan was sitting on the dresser watching her sister get out of her school clothes.

Sandra thought Joan meant the candy company.

"No, *Nessie*," said Joan.

Sandra shook her head no.

"Don't tell me you've never heard of the Loch Ness Monster," Joan said.

"I've heard the name. What is it?"

"It's this monster that lives in a lake in Scotland. It's not mean or anything, that's just what they call it, the Loch Ness Monster, 'Loch' meaning 'lake.' But they call him 'Nessie' for short."

"Joan, dear, where did you hear all this?"

"In class, from Mrs. Costello. Quit calling me 'dear.'"

"Your teacher told you there's a monster living in a lake in Scotland?"

"She was there last summer."

"She should be reported."

"She was *there*, Sandra, okay? She *went* there."

"And saw a monster in a lake."

"No, but *other* people have."

"I see."

"It looks a lot like Puff."

"Like who?"

"Puff the magic dragon."

"Oh God."

"What."

"I hate that song."

"*Why?*"

"It's a *children's* song."

"No it's not, it's really sad if you listen to it."

"I don't even know what it's *doing* on WLS."

"It's not a children's song."

"How would you know, dear?"

"It's *not*, Sandra."

"Okay."

"It's really sad."

"I said okay."

Joan sat there on the dresser swinging her legs, banging her heels, watching Sandra spray and tease her hair in front of the dresser mirror, building it up into a large helmet framing her thin face.

"Where you going?"

"Deb's."

"What're you gonna do?"

"How should *I* know?"

"Can I come?"

"Of course not."

"Please? I'll be quiet," she promised.

Sandra suddenly set down the hairbrush, hurried over to the radio, and turned up the volume.

Why does the sun go on shining?

Sandra stood there looking off.

Why does the sea rush to shore?

She sat heavily on the edge of the bed.

Don't they know it's the end of the world?

She fell back on the bed and lay there staring up.

'Cause you don't love me anymore.

She brought her hands up over her eyes.

Still sitting on the dresser kicking her feet, Joan waited for the song to end. When it finally did, Sandra sat up and sniffed and dabbed at her eyes with the back of her hand.

"Thinking about Troy?"

"Shut up, Joan."

"Sorry."

Joan was a little afraid that her sister might actually be seriously mental, the way she carried on over that song, crying over Troy Donahue as if he had stopped loving her, even though he had never started, even though Sandra had never even *met* Troy Donahue or even seen him except in movies and the photos in the magazines she was always reading.

Sandra was back at the dresser mirror, using a tissue to wipe her runny eyeliner.

"Sandra?"

"What."

"Can I ask you a personal question?"

"No. Bye." She left.

————

Before handing their papers back Mrs. Costello wanted to read a few of them to the class, the ones she thought were particularly special.

Joan was excited.

But the first one Mrs. Costello read was about someone's cocker spaniel having puppies. Then she handed the paper to its author, Marianne Landis. And the one after that was about someone's trip to Gettysburg, Pennsylvania, the site of the famous Civil War battle, and handed it back to Michael Dennison. And the one after that was about planting a carrot garden in the backyard, by Denise Webber.

And that was it.

Mrs. Costello passed the rest of the papers back. On Joan's she had written in spiky red: *Entertaining but I asked for a <u>true</u> experience, Joan. C–.*

————

Lying on her bed after reading her paper aloud to Sandra, Joan wanted her sister to be honest: Didn't she think an essay about the Loch Ness Monster saving someone's life was more interesting than an essay about growing carrots?

Sandra was lying across her bed in her quilted night-gown, over one of her magazines, her hair in huge rollers, "Sugar Shack" on the radio. "But those were *real* carrots, Joan dear."

"So? I don't even *like* carrots. They're boring."

"Not the point," Sandra said wearily, turning a page.

"So what *is*?"

Sandra looked up from her magazine. "The point is," she said sadly, "you have to grow up, sweetheart. You have to begin living in the *actual* world."

"Oh really? What about Troy? He's not actual."

"Of *course* he's actual."

"Not really."

"His actual name is Merle Johnson, he's got an actual apartment in Malibu, he drives an actual Ferrari, he has a weakness for pizza, his girlfriend's name is Suzanne and they're always fighting." She went back to her magazine. "I don't know why he even *stays* with her."

"Nessie has a weakness for tuna fish."

"Who?"

"The Loch Ness Monster. That's his nickname, 'Nessie.' I only told you a hundred times."

Sandra looked up again. "Just so I know: you're saying the Loch Ness Monster is as real as Troy Donahue. Interesting." Returning to her magazine she did the theme from *The Twilight Zone*.

"You're the one," said Joan, meaning *You're the one in the Twilight Zone*. "Troy Donahue doesn't even know you, he's never even heard of you."

"At least he exists."

"So does Nessie."

"Right, and he talks to little girls in his cave and cries because no one understands him."

"Oh, Troy, you're so dreamy."

"The great big sad little monster."

"You're so creamy."

"Poor little Nessie."

"Why don't you answer my letters, Troy? I write and tell you how much I love you and you never even—"

"*Shut up, shut up, shut up,*" cried Sandra. She flung her magazine at Joan, missing her, then buried her face in her arms and wept.

Joan took the magazine from the floor and started reading an article about Paul Anka. "Easier Said Than Done" by the Essex was on the radio now and she hummed along with it.

Sandra finally lifted her wet face. Quietly she told Joan, "I just hope and pray that when you grow up, if you ever do, you never have to go through what I'm going through, that's all."

"With Troy you mean?"

"I just hope and pray."

"Well . . . thanks," said Joan. She hoped so too. It didn't look like very much fun being mental. "How 'bout some rummy?" she offered her suffering sister. That was about the only thing they still did together anymore, card games. They used to do a *lot* of things together, but now it was down to cards, usually rummy. "Wanna play?"

"With *you*?"

"I said I'm sorry."

"No you didn't."

"All right, I'm sorry, okay? Come on. One game, Sandra." All of a sudden it seemed very important to Joan. "Please?"

Sandra shrugged. "I don't care."

Joan got the cards from the little drawer of the nightstand between their beds. They sat cross-legged on Sandra's bed. Joan dealt. They were studying their cards when "Puff the Magic Dragon" came on.

Sandra looked at Joan over her cards.

Joan said, "What."

"Nothing."

Little Jackie Paper loved that rascal Puff . . .

Sandra drew from the pile, looked at the card, and threw it away.

Joan couldn't use it, drew a card, the queen of clubs, and tried to concentrate on whether to keep it or throw it back.

Pirate ships would lower their flags when Puff roared out his name . . .

She threw it back.

"*Thank* you, my dear," said Sandra, picking it up. She laid it down along with the jack and the king of clubs, humming along with the radio, and discarded the four of hearts.

And frolicked in the autumn mist in a land called Honalee . . .

Joan stared at her cards, one end to the other, then back again.

Sandra said, "*Tick-tock, tick-tock . . .*"

"I'm trying to think, will ya?"

One gray night it happened, Jackie Paper came no more . . .

It was no use. Joan closed the fan of her cards, hung her head, and listened to the song. Sandra kept quiet. It came to the end: *So Puff that mighty dragon sadly slipped into his cave.* Joan could picture that so clearly, picture his face at the end of his long, drooping neck, his big, hurt-looking eyes. The singers did the chorus one last time: *Puff the magic dragon lived by the sea . . .*

The moment the song ended the deejay came back, talking a mile a minute, not even mentioning Puff, going on about an appearance he was making at a shopping center somewhere.

"God," Sandra said quietly.

Joan wiped her eyes. "What."

"That *is* sad."

Joan nodded and nodded at her sister: "Isn't it? Isn't it?"

They both spread open their cards again. Sandra said, "Whose turn?"

Joan sniffed. "I don't know. I think mine," she said, and threw down a card, it didn't matter which. "*His head was bent in sorrow,*" she sang to her sister.

"I heard the song, dear."

"*Green scales fell like rain . . .*"

"That's enough now," Sandra told her, and threw down the nine of diamonds.

Joan looked at it, looked at her hand. "*Ah,*" she realized, and snatched it up, laid out the nine, ten, and jack of diamonds, then sat back.

"Discard please."

Joan did so.

Sandra lifted a card from the pile. "Damn," she whispered, and threw it down.

Joan drew, feeling happy now, the game heating up, carrying them along together. She looked at the card and, pretending to be angry, flung it down.

"Temper, temper," Sandra sang, picking it up.

BIGFOOT TELLS ALL

It's not so bad *now* but when I was younger I used to spend entire days just wandering around looking for something to couple with. And I mean *anything*. I once humped a birch tree. I'm serious. *Saying* things to it: *Aw baby, you're the one, you're the one . . .*

Sad, I know.

But there was one who really *was* the one. I called her Sweet Pea, a lovely young black bear I met back east, with eyes you could drown in. And here's the kicker: *she* came on to *me*. Generally I steer clear of bears, black, white, or brown. I'm a pretty tough hombre but I don't mess with those folks. So when I stepped into a clearing one fine spring morning and there she was, I froze. Forget about trying to run away: they're quick as cougars when they want to be.

She comes walking up.

I'll be honest, I was scared.

She starts checking me out, sniffing me all over like mad—balls, butt hole, everywhere. But then all of a sudden, just like that, she quits. Goes walking away. I felt like saying, *What'm I, wolverine shit?* Sounds crazy, but I felt kind of hurt, you know? Rejected. But *then*, get this. She pads on up to a little mossy spot, bends all the way over, and looks back at me, gives me this look over her shoulder like saying, *Well? How 'bout it, handsome?*

And who am *I*, right? Who am I to argue with a horny bear?

We spent that entire spring together, me and Sweet Pea. Truly, without a doubt, the happiest three months of my entire miserable fucking life. I even gave up eating meat, just so I wouldn't have to leave her side. We lived on bugs, berries, honey, nuts, mushrooms, and love. You should have seen me, I was in fantastic shape. And at least three times a day she would turn to me with this *look* meaning *C'mere, ya big lug.*

I'm telling you, I was crazy about that bear. And I'll tell you something else, she was crazy about *me*. I know she was.

So I don't get it. To this day I do not understand.

It happened like this:

We're sitting together under a tree one afternoon near the end of spring, *sprawling* there, both of us completely exhausted after some incredible high-geared lovemaking. Then all of a sudden she starts looking at me funny, like she's wondering, *Who the hell are you?*

I said, "What's the matter, babe?"

She's up on her feet now, on her hind legs, making low, dangerous sounds.

I get up, too. "What's wrong, Sweet Pea? What is it, hon?"

She gives this loud, ugly growl like I never heard from her before and rakes her long, beautiful claws across my chest, nearly ripping out my heart, literally. Then she drops back down on all fours and goes loping away, in and out among the trees.

I'm on the ground now, yelling after her, "Sweet Pea, come back! Come back!"

She doesn't even turn.

For two whole days and nights I laid there, waiting to die, *wanting* to. By day three, though, I had some company. In the tree overhead a bunch of smug-looking vultures were waiting. I hate those motherfuckers, always have. So I got better, just to spite them.

But the *deeper* wound she gave me, that's something I don't think I'll ever recover from, not fully. She hurt me bad. And what I'd like to know is, why? What the hell was *that* about, *turning* on me like that? What did I do? Like I told you, we were just sitting there.

You know what it was like? It was like she'd been under some kind of *spell* all spring and now she'd all of a sudden woken up from it. Is that what springtime does to female black bears? Is that all it was for her, a spring fling?

I went back to eating meat with a vengeance.

I even ate one of *you* recently. I'm sorry but he had it coming. All morning the silly sonofabitch kept following me around from tree to tree, in his L. L. Bean–wear, clicking away. I pretended not to notice— just walking along, another beautiful day in paradise—meanwhile leading him deeper and deeper into the woods. Then I hurried on ahead and hid behind a large oak, waiting for him to catch up. When he did I stepped out very casually. "Oh, hello," I said. "Lovely morning, isn't it?"

The look on that man's face.

Priceless.

But I want you to know, I only meant to slap the bastard, give him a good hard slap in the face for being such a pest, but his whole fucking *head* came off. And get this, for a full five seconds he's still standing there, still upright!

I didn't know whether to laugh or scream.

Anyway, I went ahead and ate him: waste not, want not. He wasn't bad. Meat is meat, right? You're wondering did I eat the head. I did not. Brains are supposed to be good for you, but frankly I don't think this fucker had any. Afterwards, though, I borrowed his camera, took a bunch of selfies, let you people see what kind of "monster" you've been harassing all these years:

Looking off, pondering the mystery of existence . . . Click.

Smiling down at a cute little chipmunk . . . Click.

Staring into the lens with a smoldering sensuality . . . Click.

Showing outrage at man's abuse of the environment . . . Click.

Looking lonely . . . lonely . . . Click.

I hung the camera up on a low branch for someone to hopefully find and send the photos to *National Geographic*—not, if you please, the *National Enquirer*, sharing the page along with the latest Elvis sighting.

I read all your leavings.

I'm aware of the way you think of me. A freak, a tabloid freak. And you know what? Let's face it, you're right. That's exactly what I am—a freak, a fluke, a mistake of nature. Where's another like me? Nowhere. Nowhere.

But hey. Don't get me wrong. I'm not complaining. Are you kidding? With all this beauty around me? All these trees? All these birds and brooks and butterflies to wander among? Day after day after day? No, listen, I'm so happy out here I could fucking scream. In fact I often do, like this:

AAAAAAAAHHHHHHHH!

Then you can hear all creatures big and little as they scurry off into caves, into trees, into burrows. Then it's quiet. All around, it's very quiet.

And I walk on.

OTTO AND THE
AVENGING ANGEL

There once was a scrawny boy named Otto who, out of boredom, often spied on his fat aunt Mary in the shower. They lived alone in a house full of animal knickknacks, doilies with brown scorch marks, Jesus half-asleep on the cross, lots of afghans, some peacock feathers in a dusty vase, and a very loudly ticking clock on the living room wall, like drops of water on Otto's head, like Chinese torture.

School was no relief: *The capital of Alabama is Montgomery, the capital of Alaska is Juneau, the capital of Arizona is Phoenix . . .*

Otto was actually *afraid* of boredom. You could die from it, he knew. He passed *out* from boredom once, in his room. He hurt his elbow when he fell.

Aunt Mary always showered at exactly six in the evening, then afterward cooked their dinner: pork this, pork that. She never locked the bathroom door. She trusted Otto. He would wait until he heard her singing in there:

"Old MacDonald had a farm . . ."

Then he would carefully open the door and step into the bathroom. That was always the scary part, the stepping-into-the-bathroom part, so he would silently say to himself, *Otto opened the door and stepped into the bathroom,* as if he were in his room reading a story about a desperate boy named Otto stepping into the bathroom to spy on his overweight aunt in the shower.

The bathroom was already quite steamy.

"And on this farm he had some ducks . . ."

From his aunt's blurry form behind the milky curtain he could tell which way she was facing and he would tiptoe to the other side.

"With a quack-quack here and a quack-quack there . . ."

Then he would pull back a tiny bit of curtain, just enough for one eye, and stand there for a full ten seconds gazing in amazement at her glossy fatness: big fat back, big fat butt, big fat legs, and sometimes, if she turned a little, one of her big fat wobbly boobs.

"And on this farm he had some pigs . . ."

Then he would quickly tiptoe out of the bathroom, hurry to his room, collapse across the bed, and laugh and laugh at how fat and pink as a pig she was, singing away like that, no idea her dear little Otto was there. That was what tickled him the most, how she just kept singing away:

"With an oink-oink here and an oink-oink there . . ."

Then at dinner while his aunt blabbered on about this and that, he would sit there politely nodding and smiling, as if he were listening.

But then one evening as she cut up her pork chop Aunt Mary said to him, "You know, Otto, you're getting way too big to be spying on your fat old auntie in the shower, don't you think?"

Otto sat there with a forkful of mashed potato halfway to his mouth, having turned to stone.

"Would you like to know what happens to boys who behave like that?" she said. "An angel with a sword comes to their room at night and chops off their head. He chops . . . off . . . their *head*," she repeated, then ate and ate.

Otto didn't really believe an angel would come to his room and chop off his head, or even come at all. But as he lay in bed that night he stayed awake just in case, because if an angel really did come he wanted to see it, because that would be interesting, an angel.

After an hour, no angel.

After another hour, still no angel.

Just like everything else halfway interesting, there's no such thing, he thought bitterly, and turned over, facing the wall. He was on the brink of sleep when a quiet voice said, "Otto," and he flipped over.

An angel was standing there.

It was holding a broadsword at its side, its huge white wings slowly opening and closing, lifting it up and down a little. It had a soft-looking face and long, curly golden hair, but its arms were powerful looking, so Otto wasn't sure if it was a womanly man-angel or a manly woman-angel.

"Did you know," it said in a soft man-or-woman voice, "the name 'Otto' is the same spelled backwards?"

Otto sighed and said of course he knew that and asked the angel if it knew that carpenter ants can lift forty times their own weight.

The angel said that was *very* common knowledge and asked Otto if he knew Our Lord Jesus was a carpenter.

Otto asked the angel if Jesus could lift forty times His own weight.

The angel said of course He could, being the Son of God.

Otto asked the angel if it knew "God" spelled backwards was "Dog"?

The angel said, "Look, just quit spying on your auntie in the shower."

"Or else?" Otto prompted.

"Or else I'll be back."

"With what, another warning?"

"That's right, mister."

Otto gave a contemptuous little snort.

"Don't push me," the angel warned.

"You don't scare me," Otto told it. "You *bore* me."

"Is that so? Well, how's *this* for boring?" said the angel, lifting the sword in both hands above its head.

Otto turned onto his back and spread his arms. "Go ahead," he urged. He didn't care. If even an angel from Heaven was boring, there was really no hope, in this life or the next. "Do it," he said, and closed his eyes, hoping it wouldn't hurt very much.

After a minute went by and his head was still attached, he said, "Problem?"

There was no reply.

He opened his eyes.

The angel was gone.

On the floor near the bed was a tiny white feather. Otto picked it up. He studied it carefully, turning it by the shaft, trying to decide if it came from Heaven or his pillow. *What's the difference?* he thought, and flipped it away. It hung in the air a moment, then drifted down and lay on the floor.

Otto returned to his back and lay there staring up at the ceiling, at that set of cracks resembling a monkey on its hind legs flourishing either a bowling pin or a turkey drumstick.

Even here in his room with the door closed he could still hear the living room clock, like a dripping faucet. He wondered what insanity might be like. *Might be kind of interesting*, he decided, and placed all of his attention on the drops of water falling one by one, smack in the middle of his forehead.

WOLFMAN AND JANICE

"You through?" she asked him.

Sitting very straight, his face raised to the full moon, Frank held up a furry finger meaning *not quite*.

She sighed.

He gripped his knees and howled some more.

They were sitting at opposite ends of an iron patio bench, Janice in her pink terry cloth robe and slippers, a magazine open in her lap, Frank still in his shirt and tie, his face and hands and bare feet covered in thick brown fur. His right ankle was shackled and attached by a chain to a leg of the bench, with a few feet of slack. A putter and several golf balls lay close at hand.

When Frank was finally through howling he sat back, spent. "There," he said.

"Is it absolutely necessary to be quite so loud?" she asked.

He looked at her. "You trying to be funny?"

"No, Frank," she told him wearily. "Believe me."

"It's not something I can *control*. It's a . . . what's the word . . . when you can't control something you do."

"'Weakness.'"

"No, come on, what is it, it's a . . . it's a . . ." He held his head in both hands. "I can't *think* when I'm like this."

"'Compulsion,'" she told him.

He pointed at her. "Exactly. It's a compulsion. You know what a compulsion is, Jan?"

"I just gave you the word."

"All right, then."

"All I'm asking, could you possibly lower the volume a little."

"Howl quietly, you mean?" He whispered, "*Owooo.*"

She sat there looking at him. "Don't be a wiseass, Frank. On top of everything else, don't be a wiseass."

"I'm saying I can't help it."

"Being a wiseass?"

"Howling loud."

"Yeah, well . . ." She returned to her magazine. "I don't have to like it."

"Hey." He leaned toward her along the bench, jabbing at his chest. "You think *I* like this? Any of this? You think I'm having a good *time* here, Jan?"

"You're spitting on me."

He drew back, apologizing, and wiped his mouth with his necktie.

She explained to him, "The only reason I mention the volume, Mrs. Krapilowski heard you last night."

"Thought she was supposed to be so deaf."

"She got her hearing aid adjusted. She was telling me all about it."

"What'd she say?"

"It works fine now."

"About the howling, Jan. What'd she say about the howling?"

"She wanted to know if we'd gotten a dog."

"What did you tell her?"

"I told her yes, as a matter of fact we had, a very large one."

"You're kidding."

"What was I supposed to say? 'No, Mrs. K, that was just my husband, that was just Frank.'"

"Tell her to mind her own goddamn business."

"You tell her."

"I will," he said, giving his ankle a yank. "Let me out of this and I'll go over there right now."

"All right, take it easy."

"You think I'm kidding? Unlock this thing and watch me."

"You're getting worked up, Frank," she warned.

"She doesn't scare me."

"I should hope not, the woman's eighty-two years old."

"I don't care, I'll go over there right now and kick her ass."

"All right, easy, big fella."

"I'll crush . . . her fucking . . . *skull*."

Janice got to her feet and pointed down at him: "Stop it, Frank. Right now. You can stop."

He sat there breathing hard.

"Settle *down*," she commanded.

His breathing began to taper off.

"Look at me, Frank. Look at me."

"Quit bossing, will you?"

"You okay now?"

"I'm fine, I'm fine," he said irritably.

She remained standing there. "Would you like me to bring the little TV out? Do you want to watch some television?"

"No. Sit down, Jan. Please," he added.

She sat and began rummaging through a large straw bag at her feet. "I've got your *Golfer's Digest.*" She pulled out a small magazine. "You want it?"

"Is that the July issue?"

She scanned the cover. "*Uhhhh,* yes."

"Already read it."

She put it back and pulled out a stack of large Dixie cups. "Need to pee?"

"No. Listen, I'm fine, Jan." He reached down for the putter near his feet and stood up with it. "Really. I'm fine."

"All right, then." She reopened her magazine and looked for her place.

Frank set up a ball and putted toward the mouth of a Dixie cup at the other end of the patio. "Get in there," he told the ball, but it veered off. He nudged another one in place. "What're you reading?"

"Article."

"'Why Men Are Such Stupid, Brutal Slobs and Women So Intelligent, Loving, and Kind.'"

"It's a gardening magazine."

"'Why Men Are Such Lousy Gardeners and Women So—'"

"Frank?"

He putted, watched it, and shook his head. "Pathetic." He set the putter against the bench and sat down heavily. "Absolutely pathetic."

"This isn't a very good surface," she offered.

"That's not it. But thank you," he added. He sat there gazing at the moon.

She went on reading.

After a while he gave a quiet chuckle.

She looked at him. "What."

"Told her we got a dog, huh?"

She smiled. "A big'n'."

"A goddamn *wolf*hound."

They laughed together.

He was still laughing while she sat there looking down at her hands. "Frank?" she said when he was through.

"Yeah?"

"Mrs. Krapilowski also wanted to know if we'd seen her cat anywhere."

He didn't say anything.

"Remember her cat? Billy Boy? Apparently he's been missing. For a while now."

"And she's wondering if our new dog ate him?"

She looked at him. "Did you?"

"Jesus Christ, Jan."

"*Did* you, Frank?"

"In the first place, how could I? When? You've been *with* me every time, right here."

"Not that first time. I wasn't with you then. You were on your own all night."

He looked off.

She waited.

"How long's the thing been missing?" he asked.

"About three months," she told him, significantly.

"Yeah, well . . . so what if I did?"

"Aw, nice going, Frank," she said with disgust.

He turned to her. "You never even liked that cat. He used to crap on your geraniums."

"That doesn't make it okay to *eat* him, for God's sake."

"I didn't say I did. I don't know *what* the hell I did that night." He looked off again. "The last thing I remember, I was doing the dishes. That's the very last thing I remember, washing the dishes."

"Frank, we've been over this. *I* was washing, you were drying."

"Whatever."

"Then all of a sudden—"

"Yeah, yeah."

"—you flung the salad bowl against the wall, turned into a werewolf, and ran out of the house. I didn't see you again until morning."

He stared into the distance. "I remember running. I do remember that. Running through the dark, from yard to yard . . ."

"By the way, do you happen to know how *old* that bowl was?"

"Swinging myself over fences . . ."

"Are you listening to me?"

"Leaping over lawn chairs . . ."

"*Frank.*"

He snapped out of it. "What."

"I'm saying, that bowl you broke?"

"You already told me. It belonged to your grandmother."

"My *great*-grandmother. That bowl had been in our family for over a hundred—"

"Well I'm *sorry*, Jan, y'know? But I can hardly be held accountable for—"

"Wait a minute, now," she told him, a finger in the air. "*First* you threw the bowl. That was Frank.

Then you turned into a werewolf. So don't try your 'compulsion' defense on me."

"Okay, so why did I throw the bowl? Answer me that."

"I have no idea. You were putting it in the wrong cabinet—it goes in the cabinet with the punch bowl and the colander and you were putting it in with the little bowls. I happened to point it out to you, and that was it—there goes the bowl, there goes Frank."

"I can imagine how you 'pointed it out' to me."

She nodded at him. "Right. I see. So this is all *my* fault."

"I didn't say that."

"But that's what you think, isn't it. My constant bitchiness finally awakened the werewolf within. Well, I'm sorry, Frank, but I'm not taking the rap for this."

"Nobody's asking you to."

"No way, mister." She turned away, shaking her head.

"Jan . . ."

"I know I tend to be somewhat assertive—okay, *bossy*." She angrily flicked away a tear. "I'm aware of that," she said. "But dammit, *somebody* has to take charge. *Somebody* has to say, 'This is the correct way to *do* things.' We *don't*, for example, put the big salad bowl in with the *little* salad bowls. Yes, it's a salad bowl but it belongs with the *other* big items: the mixing bowl, the punch bowl, the colander. Things go in their *place*." She looked at him. "Otherwise, do you know what we have? What we end up with, Frank?"

He threw back his head and howled.

She nodded. "Exactly."

"*Owooooooo!*" he cried again.

She returned to her magazine, a hand over her Frank-side ear.

"*Ow-ow-owoooooo!*" he added.

When he was finally through he sat back, catching his breath.

Janice touched a finger to her tongue and turned a page.

"This the new dog?" asked Mrs. Krapilowski.

"Mrs. K!" said Janice, springing to her feet, spilling her magazine.

The small old woman was standing at the edge of the patio in her nightgown, leaning on her cane with both hands. "I like the beard. My late husband tried growing one but it came in all patchy. He looked like a bum, which of course he was. Yours is nice and full, though."

Frank vaguely touched his face. "Thank you."

"I would shave the forehead, though," she added, hobbling up. "*So.* What's all the howling about? *Hm?*"

Janice said, "The thing is, Mrs. K . . ."

Frank said, "I was just . . . you know . . ."

"Howling, right. My late husband used to howl quite a lot—in fact whenever he was drunk, which was most of the time—but in the *house*, with the windows closed. We didn't want to disturb the neighbors, you see. We were concerned about that. *I* was, anyway. I didn't feel we had the right to be keeping people awake with our noise. I realized how inconsiderate that would be."

"It's not that simple, Mrs. K," Janice told her.

"Oh, I know that, dear. Those were simpler times, we were simpler people, with simpler values—respect for the rights of others, for example. Quaint, old-fashioned notions like that."

"Mrs. K, Frank is a werewolf."

"I sympathize. My late husband was frequently a monster. But do you see the point I'm trying to make here? I think you're both very nice people, I really do, and I'm awfully sorry about your marital problems—I often wanted to chain *my* husband up . . ." She paused, turning slowly to Frank. "By the way," she said, "did you eat my cat?"

Frank looked over at Janice.

"Don't look at her, I'm talking to you. Did you eat my Billy Boy?"

"Not . . . as far as I know."

"What the hell is *that* supposed to mean?"

"He doesn't remember, Mrs. K."

"He doesn't remember if he ate a cat? An entire cat?" She studied Frank, who sat with his head hung. "What're we dealing with here?"

"A werewolf, Mrs. K, and he really doesn't remember."

Mrs. Krapilowski nodded at him knowingly. "My late husband used to use that one, too." She spread her arms and spoke in a whiny voice: "'How can I be blamed for something I don't even remember doing?'" She dropped her arms. "I used to tell him, 'Well, *I* remember, sweetheart, every detail,' and I *still* remember. He was a worthless drunk, a sadistic sonofabitch, and a lousy lay. But after he finally died I found myself a true companion, a trustworthy friend, a comfort in my twilight years." Approaching Frank, she spoke to his bowed head: "My own . . . dear . . . delightful . . . Billy Boy."

"Leave him alone, Mrs. K."

"Stay out of this." She poked him in the arm with her cane. "So, how *was* he? Nice and plump, huh? How'd he taste? And don't say 'Like chicken' or I'll beat you right across your ugly, stinking—"

"*Stop* it. Leave him be."

Mrs. Krapilowski pointed her cane at Janice: "Shut the hell up or you'll get the same, girlie."

With a horrible growl Frank sprang from the bench onto all fours.

"Frank, no!" Janice shouted.

He was about to take a bite out of Mrs. Krapilowski's ankle but the old woman smacked him on the head with her cane. "Get *away*, get *away*," she told him, stepping backward as he crawled after her.

"*Frank, don't, please*," Janice begged.

He crawled as far as the chain allowed and swiped at the old woman, left and right.

Mrs. Krapilowski, out of his reach, shouted at Janice, "I want him put down! He ate my Billy Boy and he tried to eat me and I want him destroyed!"

"He can't *help* himself, Mrs. K, it's a—"

"'Compulsion,' right," she said, sneeringly. "That was my late husband's *favorite* one." She did his whiny voice again: "'I can't help myself!' Yeah, bullshit. Now listen to me, both of you. I want quiet. I want peace and quiet. I'm eighty-two years old," she explained, with growing self-pity, "and I'm all alone—thanks to Dogboy here—and all I'm asking, all I would like, is to be allowed to *sleep* at night. Is that really so much to ask? I put it to you, is that really so terribly much?"

"We'll keep it down, Mrs. K," Janice told her. "I promise."

"You do that, dearie. Muzzle him, drug him, I don't care, whatever it takes—or I'm calling the dogcatcher."

Frank growled at her.

"Want some *more* of this?" she asked him, holding the cane near his face. He swiped at it but she lifted it away, saying, "*Ha*," and went hobbling off.

"Goodnight, Mrs. K," Janice called out.

"We'll see," Mrs. Krapilowski called back.

Frank, still on all fours, was growling after her, straining at his chain.

Janice stayed where she was: "Okay, Frank. It's okay now. She's gone. Let her go. Just let her go."

But he continued growling, deep in the werewolf state now.

She stepped closer, carefully. "Frank, listen to me. Are you listening?"

His growling dropped down a notch.

She knelt close to him, sitting on her heels, hands clenched in her lap. "You are not an animal," she told him in a loud voice. "Do you hear me? Do you understand? You are Frank Peterson, of the law firm Hopper, Atwell, and Peterson. You enjoy barbecuing. You have a beautiful house and a lovely wife. You're a marvelous golfer. You drive a Lexus. You're a Libra. You tend to put things in the wrong place. You're afraid of flying. You're afraid of Ronald McDonald. And you are very afraid of the dark."

He was quiet by now, though still looking off in the direction Mrs. Krapilowski had gone.

"You're Frank," she said, and helped him to his feet. "You're Frank," she repeated, returning him to the bench. They sat down at his end, close to one another. Frank stared at her. She placed her hand on his furry cheek. "You're my husband," she said. They sat there looking into one another's eyes.

Frank finally spoke: "You really think I'm a marvelous golfer?"

Janice sighed, dropping her hand. She got up heavily and returned to her end of the bench.

"No?" he said, watching her. "You were just saying that?"

She picked up her magazine.

He looked around. "Where's Mrs. K? What happened? Where'd she go?"

"Back to bed." She opened her magazine and began flipping through it indifferently.

Frank sat there staring off. "Y'know . . . I *could* be a marvelous golfer—well, maybe not *marvelous* but pretty damn decent—if I could just get my putting game down. I'll make a fantastic drive, an exquisite approach shot, I'm on the green in two, and then I'll *three*-putt." He shook his head. "Drives me nuts."

Janice quit turning pages and began slowly raising her face to the moon.

"There's an excellent piece in the *Digest* this month," Frank went on, "all about putting. I like what he says, especially this one part . . ."

Janice sat there gazing at the moon with sorrowful longing, sighing deeply.

Frank got to his feet with the putter and nudged a ball into place: "How did he put it? Something like, 'As you're about to putt, imagine a current running from your hands down the shaft to the ball, and from the ball to the hole, its inevitable destination.' I like that: 'Its inevitable destination.'" He carefully drew back the putter.

Janice began howling.

———————

Afterward they sat back, limp, utterly spent.

"*That*," he said, "was absolutely . . ."

"Wonderful," she said, taking his hand without looking.

"The way you were *harmonizing*, Jan—where'd you ever learn *that*?"

She shook her head. "It just came out."

"We were doing a damn *duet* together."

"I feel so relaxed."

They sat there holding hands, enjoying the moon.

"Beautiful-looking thing," he said, "isn't it?"

"Like a pearl."

"Or one of those giant cheese wheels."

"Swiss."

He smiled. "Right."

"That would be nice right now," she said, "wouldn't it? With some rye crackers?"

"And black olives," he suggested.

"And a nice, freshly dead animal," she added.

"There you go."

"Still warm."

"Now you're talking."

They sat there, famished.

"Maybe Mrs. K will come back," he offered.

"That would be nice," she agreed, and looked at him. "But what are *you* going to eat?"

They howled with laughter.

KUKLA

Rudy knew what *Fran* was, anyway. She was a lady, a human lady. And he liked her. He liked how pretty she was and how nice, and the way she sang in her pretty voice.

He wasn't so sure about Ollie, though, what *he* was. He thought maybe a crocodile, but his mom watched the show a lot—it was on at night—and said he was a dragon. A *nice* one, though, with sad, friendly eyes and only one big overhanging tooth in front that made him look a little goofy and stupid, which he *was* a little, also funny, the way he liked himself so much, *admired* himself, which was maybe like a dragon, how they were, except there was no such thing as dragons, or puppets either, actually. Well, there were puppets but they weren't *alive*: someone had to make them move and say things. So maybe Ollie wasn't a dragon *or* a crocodile, just a puppet with long jaws and sad eyes and a big front tooth.

Kukla, though.

When he asked his mom about Kukla, she wasn't sure: "A little clown?"

He did have a big ball for a nose like a clown, along with two big spots of rouge on his cheeks. He also had surprised-looking eyebrows and a little circle for his mouth so he looked like he was always saying "Oh no!"

"Or a little boy?" his mom said.

Except, he was *bald*, on top anyway, with hair along the sides like Uncle Seymour had. And anyway, if he was supposed to be a little bald-headed boy he didn't *sound* like one—he sounded like a girl, and acted like one, fussy about stuff, like a fussy girl. Sometimes he even scolded Ollie for not being fussy enough, for being a little thick, which Ollie was, but at least he wasn't like Kukla—he wasn't scary. Kukla reminded Rudy of Jerome Sawyer in his class, who acted like a girl the way he swung his arms when he walked and the way his hands got fluttery when he talked and the high, tinkly way he laughed, pressing his hand to his chest like an actress.

But Rudy didn't *hate* Jerome, like some of the others did, some of the other boys. They hated him and beat him up a lot. And the way Jerome would cry! So *loud*. Not even caring he was crying like that, like a girl would cry, which made them even madder, so they beat him up some more, making him cry even worse.

Rudy was more *scared* of Jerome than mad at him. Which he didn't understand, because how could he be scared of someone who was like a girl? Why would he be scared of a girl? But he was scared of Jerome the same way he was kind of scared of Kukla, who wasn't even real, who was just a puppet who was like a little fussy boy with a girl's voice wearing makeup and little white mittens.

Sometimes Rudy wanted to see Ollie go *after* Kukla, knock him down when Kukla started carrying on in that voice, make him stop *being* like that. Which was how he always felt when they beat up Jerome. He felt sorry for him but also glad because maybe it would help him be less girly, less scary. That's what they were trying to do, the other boys, trying to beat the girl out of him.

But Rudy had to admit: he liked to watch Jerome on the ice.

Everyone else at the pond just skated around or played crack-the-whip or else played hockey over on the hockey side, but Jerome would *figure* skate. It shocked Rudy how good he was. Sometimes people would stand around in a wide circle watching him do figure eights and jump in the air and whirl around and land on one skate and sail backward with his arms out like wings and a faraway look on his face. People said if he kept on like this he was going to be in the Olympics someday.

One night Rudy had a dream that Jerome was at the pond doing his usual tricks, but he was also Kukla, with white mittens, rouge, and high eyebrows, his little round lipsticked mouth whistling a tune he skated to, the "Here We Are Again" song they always played at the start of the show, flipping his hips like a show-offy girl. Then the hockey players broke into the circle of watchers and were at him, beating him with their sticks, Jerome screaming "*Nooooo*" through his Kukla mouth, going down gracefully, like a ballerina, and lying there while they kept on beating him, swinging their sticks like chopping wood, till Jerome started coughing up strands of grey puppet-stuffing, then twitched all over, and was dead. Then everyone could relax.

When Rudy saw Jerome at school the next day he wanted to warn him not to go skating, or anyway *figure* skating. But no boy ever spoke to Jerome, otherwise people would think you didn't mind the way he was, or that you even *liked* the way he was, secretly being that way yourself.

There *was* one thing Rudy would like to ask Jerome: Did he watch *Kukla, Fran and Ollie*, and if he did, who was his favorite, Kukla?

> *Dear Kukla,*
> *You are just a puppet but I wish you were my friend.*
> *Love,*
> *Jerome Sawyer*

Rudy wouldn't mind writing to Fran:

> *Dear Fran,*
> *You are very nice, also very pretty, especially when*
> *you sing.*
> *Sincerely,*
> *Rudy Petrovitch*

But she would probably write back:

> *Dear Rudy,*
> *Glad you enjoy the show.*
> *Best wishes,*
> *Fran Allison*

Actually, his *mom* enjoyed the show more than he did. Sitting behind him on the couch she would give out little laughs at the three of them and say how "clever" they were, and he would feel proud. She never watched any of his other puppet shows, though. She never watched *Howdy Doody*, for example. She didn't think Howdy or Buffalo Bob or Clarabell were clever. Rudy thought they were *very* clever, especially Clarabell when he ran around squirting everyone with water. That was clever. But Kukla, Fran, and Ollie never got like that, rowdy and fun like that. But he still liked to watch them, hearing his mom laugh at something clever they said, and he liked Fran an awful lot, and Ollie with his one big goofy tooth.

But Kukla.

One evening during a commercial he asked his mom on the couch behind him what she thought of Kukla, how she felt about him, if she liked him.

"Well . . . he's a puppet, hon."

"I know, but do you like him?"

"Sure. He seems nice."

"Would you ever want to hit him?"

"Hit him?"

"Would you?"

"Why would I want to hit him?"

"Or see Ollie hit him? Or Fran? Or *somebody*?"

"No, I wouldn't. Why? Would you?"

He didn't answer.

"Rudy?"

"What."

"Would *you* like to hit Kukla?"

"Sometimes."

"Why? Does he bother you?"

"Sometimes."

"He's just a little puppet, hon."

"I know but why does he have to act like that?"

"Like what? How does he act?"

"Like a girl."

After a second or two she said, "Like a sissy, you mean."

He nodded.

"Well . . . maybe he *is* a sissy," she said.

He turned around and looked at her.

She shrugged.

The show came back. Kukla started carrying on in a high, excited voice about a birthday party he was planning for Beulah the witch, bringing his little white mittens together at how *nice* it was going to be. And instead of hitting him, Ollie and Fran agreed it was going to be nice, in fact a *wonderful* party.

But You Scared Me the Most

I heard something, a thump, a thud. It woke me right up. I laid there very still, my heart banging away, and listened.

Nothing.

I looked at the clock: 2:53 AM.

I listened some more.

Nothing.

I'd been asleep on my good ear, so it must have been pretty loud, although actually I *felt* it more than heard it, a thud, like something fell, something heavy, like a man tripping over the ottoman in the living room and landing with a thud, lying there very still now, holding his breath, listening to see if he woke someone up.

I wanted to yell out to him that it's only an old woman in here, only an old, frightened woman. Just take what you want—that cuckoo clock on the wall is a genuine antique, and some of those knickknacks ought to be worth something, a couple of them are Hummels. Just don't take the television. Don't take my shows.

I laid there listening.

If only Logan and Briscoe were here. Those are the cops I like on *Law & Order* reruns. "You're coming with us, pal," Logan would tell him. "You have the right to remain silent . . ." Afterwards back at the station Brisco would tease Logan about the way that old lady was looking at him, *gazing* at him.

I listened some more.

Still nothing.

My late husband had hair like Logan's—nice, thick, dark hair like that, gray in his later years of course, but still nice and thick. Kind of hard to imagine George as a cop, though. Such a timid man. Very tall, very timid. He would be praying now. He wasn't a religious person, but in any kind of crisis he would right away turn to God, not for strength or courage but for God to *take care* of it. Right now he'd be asking Jesus to please get rid of whoever might be out there. Meanwhile, you know what *I* would be doing? I'd be throwing on my robe and going out there to see what the hell the noise was. I was never scared with George around. He was always scared enough for both of us.

But now I am. Now I'm scared.

He's still being very quiet out there, lying very still, listening to me listening to him listening to me.

Oh stop it, I told myself. *There's no one out there and you know it, otherwise you'd be dialing 911, but you're not, because you know you're being silly. Something fell, that's all. Things do that, they fall. Go back to sleep where you belong. Go on. You're tired. Old and tired. Very old, very tired, very . . . very . . .*

I went out there and turned on the light and, sure enough, there was someone lying on the floor.

"Get up, you."

He got up and pulled the nylon stocking off his face. It was George.

"Oh, for *heaven sake*," I said.

"Did I wake you?"

"Of course you woke me. Is that one of mine, by the way?"

He handed back the nylon stocking.

"George, what are you doing here?"

He shrugged his bony shoulders.

"Don't you like it there?" I asked. "Are they feeding you? You look terrible."

"I'm dead, Ellen."

"You should still eat."

"Is there anything good on TV?"

Every channel had the same thing: me and George sitting on the couch staring back at me and George sitting on the couch.

"Try the Playboy Channel," he said.

"We don't have that."

"Try it."

It was me and George sitting naked on the couch staring back at me and George sitting there naked.

I turned it off.

"I wish you could see your face!" he said, pointing at me, and went staggering naked around the room, his wiener swinging, laughing like a damn fool, tripping over the ottoman, landing with a thud.

I woke up again.

I laid there very still, listening, my heart banging away painfully.

I remembered the dream I just had.

George, you bastard, I thought. *You sneak away in your sleep, not even a goodbye after forty-one years, and then come back while I'm asleep and laugh at me? Do you know how many times I could have laughed at you, George? How many times I could have flapped my elbows, going "bawk, bawk, bawk" in your pitiful, frightened face? But I never did. You know why? Because I loved you. Did you love me? Did you, George? Ever? Really?*

I was crying now.

"You bastard," I said out loud, and got up and threw on my robe and went out there, hoping it was him so I could say it to his face. I turned on the overhead. Nothing. No one.

Then another thud.

This one hurt. It nearly knocked me over. I sat on the couch. My left arm felt numb, the fingers tingling. The other phone was right there. But if I called, there would be men rushing in with a bed on wheels, strapping me down, slapping an oxygen mask on my face, wheeling me out, sliding me into the back of the van, racing away, dodging traffic, the siren screaming. I'd never make it through all that.

I sat there trying to breathe normally, trying to be not having a heart attack, wishing George was here so he could be scared and I could be brave about it. He'd probably be praying, *Please dear Jesus, don't let Ellen die, don't take her away, don't leave me here alone, let me go first.*

You bastard.

George got his wish a year ago last month, April the twenty-third. He went to bed early that night. He usually stayed up with me for *Law & Order*, but he said he felt tired. When I came into the bedroom I whispered, "George? Are you asleep?" Then I smelled his poop. I knew he had to be dead.

At the wake he looked better than ever, everyone said so. Except, his mouth had kind of a sarcastic expression to it. George had never been a sarcastic sort of person but now he looked like he was thinking, *What a joke.* I didn't know whether he meant what a joke death was, or life. His life. *Our* life.

I know we could have watched a lot less television. But at least we watched together. If something was funny we would glance at each other as we laughed, or if it was sad enough we would even hold hands. And if it was really scary George would go into the kitchen and I would yell out what's happening: *"He's still walking up the stairs . . . still walking . . . still . . . oh God somebody's stabbing him, he's falling backwards down the stairs, he's at the bottom, someone's on top of him stabbing him over and over. Okay, commercial."* And he would come back.

Sexy scenes were a problem, though. Sometimes I would tell the fondling couple, "All right, we get the point," trying to make light of it, but usually we just sat there, embarrassed, and waited it out. I often wondered if George would still be embarrassed if I wasn't there, if maybe he *liked* watching people fondle and kiss, especially on TV where all the women were skinny and beautiful instead of dumpy and ugly like his wife. But I don't think so. I think George was embarrassed about having a body at all. He's probably very happy now, fluttering around up there.

I'm not saying we never had sex. We did have separate beds, but every couple weeks or so, after lights out, George would say, "Ellen?" And I would come over. Afterwards I would go back. I would like to have been a mother but it never happened, I don't know whose fault. Anyway, after I went back to my own bed George would start talking. He was usually very quiet but now for some reason he would go on and on, usually about work, so most of it I didn't understand. He was a draftsman, all numbers, lines, and angles. I would try to stay awake, but I don't think it mattered to him very much.

My arm is starting to return. Still some tingling in the fingers, though.

George worked in the same office with the same company all the years we were married, but I only saw him there once. I was downtown Christmas shopping—this was maybe ten years ago now—and afterwards I thought what the hell and grabbed a cab outside of Marshall Field's and headed over to George's building on Wacker, took an elevator up to his floor, where a woman at a desk directed me down a nicely carpeted hallway, third door on the left. The door was open.

And there he was, sitting at his desk bending low over a large sheet of paper, with a pencil and ruler.

"George?" I said to him.

He lifted his head.

There isn't any Halloween mask half as scary as the face that looked up at me. It wasn't misshapen or anything like that. It was perfectly in place, perfectly calm, and perfectly cold—like I could have been a perfect stranger, like I *was* one, in fact.

"It's *me*, George. Your wife," I said. "Remember?"

"*Ellen*." He stood straight up, his chair rolling all the way back to the wall.

"Just checking up on you," I said, stepping in. "Mind if I sit a minute?" There was another chair and I took a load off, my shopping bags on either side. "So. What are we working on?"

He tried to explain. I tried to listen. When he was through I told him about shopping, how crowded, and about my taxi driver, some Arabian maniac, George meanwhile shooting little glances at the shopping bags. I wagged my finger at him, telling him Santa doesn't *like* little boys who peek. He giggled, pulling his bony shoulders up around his ears, back to being George, *my* George.

But there was that one moment.

And do you know what worries me? Maybe it's silly, but do you know what worries me? When I get up there and we finally meet again, I'm worried that he'll look at me like that, like he did for that one moment, like I could be anybody. *George*, I'll say to him, *it's me! Ellen! I made it!* And he'll nod, and smile politely, and fly off.

My arm is back, and the tingling in the fingers is gone. I'm going back to bed. I don't think I'm going to die tonight. But I'll be there soon, George, I'm sure. Meanwhile, be happy, dear. But not completely.

Saint Fred

One February morning in the last year that the Mass was said in Latin at Queen of Apostles parish, tiny, elderly Sister Alice Marie asked her eighth graders for a volunteer to fetch a pair of bookends from the library down the hall. She looked around at all the waving arms before finally pointing at someone.

"Fred. You go."

Feeling special, Fred got up and headed out of the room, then down the dim hallway swinging his arms, enjoying the cool air of freedom while it lasted.

The library was a very small one. Father Dillon was in there, alone, sitting at the table with a thin black book.

"Good morning, Father."

"Close the door, Fred."

Fred closed it, explaining his mission.

Father told him to sit down for a minute.

Fred sat across from him, a cold spot in his stomach.

Father closed his book and folded his hands over it. "I spoke with Father Rowley this morning. You've been serving six o'clock Mass for him this week, isn't that right?"

"Yes, Father."

"Along with . . . Alex Koenig, is it?"

"Yes, Father."

Father nodded. Then he said, "Fred?"

"Yes, Father?"

"I would like you to recite the Confiteor for me."

Fred's shoes filled with sweat. "Right now, Father?"

"Would you do that for me please?"

He couldn't. He had never learned it. It was such a *long* prayer. But you said it with your head bowed all the way down, so you could just mumble until your partner was through. It was all Latin anyway and nobody knew what it meant except Father and God, and Fred was pretty sure God didn't mind, not very much anyway, given some of the other things people did, murder for example.

Father was waiting.

Fred gave it a shot. He looked down and said quietly, "*Confiteor deos*," and then began mumbling rapidly.

"Stop."

He stopped.

"Do you know what the word 'confiteor' means?" Father asked him.

"No, Father."

"It means 'I confess.' Do you confess, Fred?"

He looked up.

Father leaned over the table toward him. "Do you confess to not knowing the Confiteor? To faking it?

Faking the Confiteor? In front of the priest? In front of the congregation? In front of God? Do you?"

"Yes, Father."

"Yes Father, what."

"Yes, Father, I confess."

Father drew back and studied him, his head to one side.

Fred looked down again.

Father said, "Do you have any idea what an honor, what a privilege, what a . . . sacred privilege it is to serve Holy Mass? Do you have any idea?"

"Yes, Father."

"You do?"

"No, Father."

"You don't?"

"I don't know, Father."

Fred heard him sigh, and looked up. "I'm sorry, Father."

Father nodded. "I'm sorry too, Fred. I'm very sorry. But I'm afraid I have to tell you: I don't think you're worthy to serve Mass. Frankly, I don't think you're altar-boy material."

Fred began crying a little, surprising himself. For one thing, he was thirteen. Also, he didn't really care very much about being an altar boy, especially the hours, and in fact he'd been wondering lately if there was something like an honorable discharge available. But the way Father told him he wasn't altar-boy material made him feel like such a failure, not only as an altar boy but as a person, as a human being.

"Father, I'll learn it. I'll memorize it. I promise."

Father shook his head no.

"I *promise*, Father."

"I think you should go back to your room now," Father told him, and opened his little book again.

Fred sat there.

"Go on," Father told him without looking up.

Fred got up and trudged to the door. But then he remembered. "Father, I'm supposed to bring back some bookends. Do you know where they are?"

"That's all right."

"Sister wanted them."

"Go on back, Fred."

Something rose up inside of him. "She sent me here to get them, Father. She *picked* me."

Father got up from his chair. "Return to your classroom. Now."

Fred's legs felt wobbly but he stood his ground: "She *chose* me, Father."

Father smiled, sadly. "Sister doesn't need any bookends, Fred. She didn't choose you. I told her to send you here."

"She asked for a *volunteer*."

Father shook his head with that sad, insulting little smile. "She didn't wish to embarrass you in front of the others, that's all. She was just being kind. Go on back now. Go on."

He went back.

———

Fred began noticing other things he faked besides the Confiteor.

Little things.

Drying the dishes, for example. His mother would wash and he would supposedly wipe, but not really:

he would just make a few rapid passes with the dish towel and put the thing away, the plate or whatever, still wet. Or the fake way he cleaned his room, kicking stuff under the bed or into the closet. Or at school while Sister was explaining long division or the Trinity, he would sit there nodding his head as if he were actually listening. Or coming back after recess: limping, rolling his head around, eyes half closed, as if he'd been in six different fights out there, in case Jean Galloway happened to be looking. He even caught himself doing things to fake *himself* out. Drinking a bottle of strawberry pop, for example, he would give a phony "*Ahhh*" after every sip, to show himself how good it was, how much he was enjoying this delicious bottle of strawberry pop, which he *was* enjoying, but not *that* much.

He began wondering if everything he *did* was fake.

That was a scary thought. That was a very scary thought.

He ended up turning to Jesus, the one person he knew he couldn't fake out. *Lord, help me try to be more sincere*, that was his prayer throughout the day. And at night he would kneel on the floor beside his bed, raise his face, and spread his arms out wide, like someone in a holy card: *Lord, help me, help me . . .*

He began going to confession every Saturday, always choosing Father Dillon's box. "Bless me, Father, for I have sinned," he would whisper into Father's ear behind the grate. But by now he was getting to be so upright, honest, and sincere he didn't have any sins to confess, mortal or venial. So he would mention faults, usually some little fake thing he caught himself doing, some little leftover phoniness: "Father, I was playing touch football and caught a pass and threw myself on the ground to make it look like a *diving* catch and then I kept rolling over and over."

Father would sigh, knowing who it was by now.

"I think I rolled over three times, Father, possibly four."

Father would tell him to go in peace and slide shut the little window, hard.

———————

One night, sure enough, Jesus appeared in his room, holding up two fingers, smiling gently. Fred knew this was only his imagination, but he also knew Jesus was *helping* him imagine, inspiring him. So he listened carefully.

Hello, Fred.

Hello, Jesus.

Congratulations on the way you've turned yourself around.

Thank you, Lord.

Keep up the good work.

I will, Lord. You know I will.

Attaboy. The other thing I came to say, I want you back serving Mass. You're definitely altar-boy material now, in fact almost priest material. So I want you to go see Father Dillon. Tell him Jesus sent you.

He won't believe me.

Probably not.

He doesn't like me very much, Lord.

I've noticed that.

He thinks I'm a fake.

He's jealous, Fred.

Of me, Lord?
Of your saintliness. It's eating him up.
Lord, I'm not a saint, not even close.
Spoken like a true saint.

———————

"Father will see you now," the squat little rectory lady told him, and stood by Father Dillon's open door, her arm showing him in.

Father was sitting behind a large, polished desk, nothing on it but a green blotter with shiny leather corners and a pen in a holder. His hands were folded on the blotter, his head to one side, with the little smirk he always had for Fred, as if he saw right through him, as if Fred amused him.

"Good afternoon, Father."

"What can I do for you, Fred?"

"Father, I would like to get back into altar boys if I could. I think I'm ready now. I've memorized the Confiteor and . . . well, I've changed my ways, completely."

Father shook his head. "I'm sorry."

That was quick.

Fred continued standing there.

Father asked him if there was anything else.

"May I say something, Father?"

"Go right ahead."

"Our Lord appeared to me last night."

"Is that right."

"He said I should try and get back into altar boys, that I should ask you about it."

"I'm sorry, Fred, but I don't believe you."

"He said you wouldn't."

Father stood up. "Enough." He pointed toward the door. "Out you go."

Fred walked to the door, then turned around. "I'll pray for you, Father."

"Out."

———

Fred began getting up every morning in time to make seven o'clock Mass, the one Father Dillon always ran. There were never many people, so he was able to sit right in the middle of the front pew. He was receiving the Eucharist each day as well, and as he waited at the altar he kept his eyes on Father, whose mouth always slid to the side when he saw Fred kneeling there. "*Corpus Domini nostri*," Father would pronounce, having no choice, as he placed the wafer on Fred's tongue, the altar boy holding the paten under his chin in case of crumbs. The altar boy was never anyone saintly or even close to it, yet there he was, in his cassock and surplice, while here was Fred in his school uniform. It wasn't fair, it wasn't right. He hated Father Dillon.

But as he returned to his pew all his anger would dissolve along with the host in his mouth, the sweet, loving mercy of Jesus seeping into his heart, and he would kneel and pray for Father Dillon, asking Our Lord to help Father get over this notion he had about Fred, that he was some kind of phony, some kind of fake saint:

Lord, help him to understand.

———

Meanwhile Fred's mother was becoming concerned, since along with attending daily Mass he'd also begun speaking to her kindly and sympathetically and had even begun doing what he could to help around the house.

"All right, Fred, what's going on?" she finally asked him one day, after coming home from work to find him mopping the kitchen floor.

"Just thought I would get this, save you the trouble."

It was just the two of them, his father having died in Korea a month after Fred was born. She had a photo of him in his army uniform on the lamp table in the living room, his hat tilted back, flashing a slanted, handsome smile. Fred knew it was hard for her: she was a real estate agent and had to look spiffy and maintain a perky attitude and she wasn't all that spiffy and perky a person.

She stood there watching him mop the floor. "Is there something you want to tell me, Fred? Something you want to talk about, that I should know?"

"Actually, Mom, there is." He stopped mopping and looked at her. "Jesus loves you."

She sighed, wearily. "Fred . . ."

He went back to mopping. "He really does, Mom."

One person who had no doubts at all about Fred's saintliness was his teacher, Sister Alice Marie. She was very old and rather feeble but could see what Jesus saw: how completely Fred had turned himself toward Heaven. She began finding excuses to keep him after school, to unpack some books or wash the blackboard or even help her check math papers. Fred was glad to oblige. He enjoyed the way she looked at him, as if he was giving off a soft light.

One day after school while he was finishing up washing the blackboard Sister asked him if he'd ever seen Jesus.

Fred told her, casually, "He comes to my room now and then, Sister, usually late at night."

"Oh, I knew it," she said, and brought her small hands together. "And what does He say to you, Fred?"

"Mostly just, you know, keep up the good work."

Sister shook her head. "How wonderful, how wonderful."

"It really is, y'know?" he said. "When you think about it."

She asked him shyly, "Has He ever . . . possibly . . . mentioned me?"

Fred gave her what she wanted: "He told me I was very lucky to have someone like you for a teacher."

"Oh, Fred, He said that?"

"He did, Sister."

Her cup began running over, which he found a little disgusting, so he made the sign of the cross in the air, blessing her, and got out of there.

Walking home he was beaten up by Jerry Klinkhammer, but not very badly. Once Klinkhammer saw Fred wasn't going to resist, he lost interest.

———

Fred held on to his sainthood through the summer, and naturally he wished to attend the Catholic high school, St. Anthony's, in the fall. The teachers there were mostly priests—not Dominicans, like Father Dillon, but Jesuits, known for their intelligence—but his mother didn't have the money, not even close to it. So he had to attend Jefferson, which was huge, and you had to be in a different classroom every period, with five minutes to find it, and he kept getting lost. He hated walking in late, so he often ended up in one of the bathrooms sitting in a stall, praying to Our Lord to help him find the way.

Our Lord said maybe if he didn't go following Vanessa Hennesey around the halls like a little panting dog, he would find his room in time.

This was something new: this banging of his heart whenever he saw her, this dry mouth, this clamminess, this urgent stirring in his pants, this boner. She was in his first-period history class, so impure looking with her black eyeliner and wild red hair, her gypsy fortune-teller clothes, bangles on her wrists, and the way she strode through the hallway swinging her long, skinny, freckled arms, never carrying books, a brazen look on her painted face. She was a harlot. That was the word the Bible used for girls like her. A harlot.

Fred loved that word.

You harlot, he would tell her from his bed at night.

He pictured her standing there, hands on her hips, tossing back her head, laughing her brazen harlot's laugh.

Please, Lord, make her go away?

Please, Lord, please? she would say, mocking him.

You harlot.

She laughed and took off all her clothes.
You filthy harlot.

————

In the confessional box one Saturday he said to Father Dillon quietly, "Bless me, Father, for I have sinned."

Recognizing Fred's voice, Father sighed.

"Father . . . I committed an impure act with myself."

Fred waited.

Father finally spoke: "That is a very grave sin," he whispered. "Our Lord hates that sin very much. Do you know why?"

"Yes, Father."

"You do?"

"No, Father."

"You don't?"

"I don't know, Father."

"I'll tell you why. Because the body is a temple of the Holy Spirit, and you have defiled that temple. Do you know what the word 'defile' means?"

"I'm pretty sure, Father."

"It means to take something pure and holy and make it foul and loathsome. Do you know what the word 'loathsome' means?"

"Yes, Father. I do."

Father let him kneel there crying.

"All right, don't overdo it."

"I'm *not*," he said.

"And *don't* raise your voice at me. Who do you think you are?"

He knew Father was waiting for him to apologize. He let Father wait.

"Do you want forgiveness or not?" Father asked him.

"Yes," he said.

"Yes, what."

"Yes, Father."

"All right, then. Pray the rosary. Pray night and day. Pray to Our Lady. *She's* the one most deeply offended by your sin. Try to imagine the way Our Blessed Mother feels while watching what you do to yourself."

"She watches, Father?"

"Of course she does, and it makes her sick. Now say a sincere Act of Contrition and go in peace," he said, sliding shut the little grate in Fred's face.

Asshole, Fred thought, and left without bothering to say an Act of Contrition.

Walking home, hands jammed in his coat pockets, dead leaves everywhere, he knew he wouldn't be back. He wasn't going to quit thinking about Vanessa Hennesey or quit defiling himself, so why pretend to be sorry? *Let Father Dillon win*, he thought, *who cares?* It was time to move on.

In his bed that night while Our Lady watched with loathing, covering her eyes but peeking through the fingers, Fred whispered like a prayer, "Vanessa . . . Vanessa . . . oh, Vanessa . . ."

SELF-PORTRAIT WITH WINE

I don't know what came over me, I really don't.

The name's Ray Parisi. You may have heard of me, probably not. I'm an artist. I do mostly portraits, with crayons and a pencil eraser. The effect is quite unique. Sometimes I think I might be another Francisco Goya. Other times I think I'm a loser who thinks he's another Francisco Goya.

Last night I was up until two in the morning doing a self-portrait in front of the dresser mirror, with some wine. Which is another thing about me, I drink too much. But so did a lot of great painters. But so do a lot of winos. Anyway, I went to bed thinking I had something pretty good this time, something pretty damn excellent in fact.

This morning? Not so sure.

It seems like every portrait I do, whether it's of myself or somebody from a magazine, it ends up looking like some kind of a monster. I never *mean* it, that's just the way they always seem to come out. Which isn't necessarily a bad thing, you know? I can imagine somebody, some art critic for a major magazine for example, writing something like *Parisi has the rare ability to capture the dark essence of his subject, what might be called the Monster Within.*

Anyway, I couldn't decide whether to feel good or bad about last night's work, and the more I studied it the more hungover I felt, so I finally gave up and got dressed and went out. It was a beautiful morning, the first really nice day of spring, with that smell in the air, that hopeful smell. I started feeling better. I started thinking about doing a monster series. I wouldn't use the word "monster" though, I'd be very dry about it, just call it Portraits. Let the *critics* come up with the idea of monsters, you see. Like I said, the air had that hopeful smell.

Then along comes this guy.

If you saw him, you would think okay, great big blustery guy in a blue business suit talking loud on one of those little bitty phones, so what? But the closer he got, the more I felt like I was being canceled out, know what I mean? Like I wasn't just a nobody but a *nothing*, like I didn't even fucking *exist*. And so, just as he was about to march on by without any sign whatsoever that *I* was here too—on this sidewalk, on this sunny morning, on this planet, this journey—in order to keep myself from being utterly rubbed out I reached over, grabbed the phone from his hand, and went tearing down the sidewalk.

Sometimes you do things and you can hardly believe you're doing them.

I told whoever was on the other end what was going on, shouting into the bottom part, saying I had just liberated the phone—that's the word I used, "liberated"—and was heading down Columbus Avenue, approaching High Street. "*Over,*" I said, and put it to my ear, then realized that was probably dumb, saying "Over," but believe it or not I never talked on one of those things before. When you had it up to your ear the bottom part didn't even reach your mouth, not even close.

"Who is this?" a young-sounding woman said in my ear. "What's going on?"

"I'm about to cross High Street now!" I shouted, and ran across without even looking, a car braking and honking at me. "That was close," I told her.

"Would you please identify yourself please?"

"Hang on a second," I said, Fatfuck still in hot pursuit, calling me names, things I won't repeat, everyone looking, so I put my head down and ran even harder, and when I looked back again he was all the way at the other end of the block, standing there bent over with his hands on his knees, out of breath, out of shape. Me, I'm in good shape. I stay up practically every night drinking and smoking and I can still outrun anyone out here, especially some lard-ass in a suit and tie. I slowed down to a trot and put the phone to my mouth again. "Hello? Still there?" I said, and put it to my ear.

"Will you kindly tell me who this is please?"

Walking now, I told her my name and a little bit about myself: between jobs at the moment, living in a room on Stevens Avenue—a "garret" I called it—and about my work, about this series I was planning to do, exploring the Monster Within. But that's not the title, I explained to her. "I'll leave that to the critics," I said. "They like titles. They *need* them. Helps them understand," and gave a little laugh. I can be charming as hell when I want.

"Where is Mr. Soderstrom?"

"Who?"

"David. The owner of the phone you're using."

I told her David was out of the picture. And he was, he was gone. "Probably to his office," I told her. "Mister Bigshot, right?" She still didn't seem to fully comprehend what was going on here, so I explained it all over again.

"You stole David's phone?"

"Mistakes were made on *both* sides," I said.

"Right out of his *hand*?"

"Hey, I'm an artist. I'm pretty deft."

"*I said, you stole David's phone right out of—*"

"I said I'm *deft*, not deaf."

We were both quiet then for a moment.

"I don't believe this," she said.

"Believe it, honey."

"Don't call me that."

"Sorry. What *should* I call you? I gave you *my* name. 'Ray,' in case you forgot."

She didn't say anything.

"Hello?" I said.

"It's Alice."

I nodded. "That's a good name. I like that. 'Alice.' Do you feel like you're in Wonderland, Alice? Talking to the Mad Hatter? I'm kidding. I'm not mad—in the sense of crazy, I mean. Or in the sense of angry, although I do sometimes get angry, especially when I witness man's inhumanity to man. That always pisses me off. Anyway, listen, might as well go for broke here, I was wondering if you'd be interested in a cup of coffee, Alice."

"Jesus."

"On me."

"You don't get it, do you."

"Is this about the phone? Are we back to that?"

"We never left it."

"Listen, he's probably got about three or four of them. He strikes me as the type."

"Type, what type? You don't even know him."

"I know he's a big fat arrogant blowhard, I know *that*. I don't like him, Alice. I'm sorry. I don't know what your connection is, if he's your boyfriend or what, but I don't care for the man, in fact I think he's the worst thing to come along. In *fact*? I might include him in my monster series. Call it simply *Man with Phone*. What do you think?"

"He's not my boyfriend, he's my boss."

"Ah. Interesting. So. Is he back yet?"

"No."

"So you must be, what, at your desk?"

"Amazing."

"You're prob'ly like a, what, a secretary or something?"

"Administrative assistant."

"So, what were you talking about, the two of you, before I so rudely interrupted. Anything interesting?"

"God," she said.

"You mean like does He exist or is this all just a cosmic accident—that what you mean?"

"I mean God as in 'God, get a *life*, will you?'"

That hurt. That really did. I stopped walking. I let my hand drop. I stood there looking around. As usual, everyone was on their way somewhere, except for me. Sometimes that makes me feel superior, like they're all just a bunch of robots and I'm the only one with an actual human soul. Other times it makes me feel adrift, you know? Like I got no direction, no purpose. That's how I felt right now. And panicky. I'll be thirty-five years old next month and look at me.

I started walking fast, towards this bar on State Street, called The Wit's End, good name for it. I had enough on me for three beers and I could probably talk my way to a fourth. I almost forgot about Alice, then I heard her voice in my hand going, "*Hello? Hello?*"

I put it up to my mouth again. "Listen," I told her, "I have to go. I have to *be* somewhere, okay? I'm sorry. It was nice talking to you, Alice."

I was trying to figure out which button to press to hang up but I could hear Alice yelling, "Wait! Don't get off! Hello? *Hello?*"

"Right here," I told her. "What's the matter?"

"Um, look," she said, "I'm going to put you on hold for a second, okay? Just for a second."

"I'm kind of in a hurry here, Alice."

"You can keep walking. I'll just be a second, okay? Roy?"

"The name's *Ray*. Ray Parisi."

"I'll be right back, Ray. So don't hang up."

"Why not?"

"Well . . . *because*. I want to talk to you some more."

"What for?"

"Get to know you better. I thought we were hitting it off, didn't you?"

"You told me to get a life, Alice."

"I was joking. That's what I do when I *like* someone, I kid around like that."

"It hurt my feelings."

"I'm sorry."

"Made me feel like a . . . you know . . ."

"A loser, right."

"I'm not a loser, Alice."

"Of course you're not."

"I told you about that series I was planning, right? About the Monster Within?"

"Sounds like a plan to *me*, Roy."

"*Ray.*"

"Listen, hang on, okay? I'll be right back. Okay?"

I told her I'd wait.

Music came on, violins playing "Somewhere My Love." As I walked along I sang quietly, "*Somewhere, my love, there will be birds to sing. Somewhere, my love, there will be birds to sing. Somewhere, my love—*"

"Hi. Still there?"

"That was quick."

"I told you."

"What did you have, another call?"

"That's it."

"Hey, I know how it is. Used to work in an office myself, wore a tie, the whole bit. Couldn't take it, Alice. Couldn't play the game. Know what I mean, the game?"

"Right. Hey, listen—"

"In fact? I might as well tell you right now before we go any further: as I mentioned, I'm an artist. And you know what that means? I'm *out* there. On the edge, Alice. Know what I'm saying?"

"The edge, right."

"So if that's a little too scary, if somebody in a suit and tie, somebody safe—somebody like David, for example—is more your type, well, we should probably forget about it right now before somebody gets hurt. Understand what I'm trying to say?"

"You mentioned a cup of coffee?"

I looked straight up at the blue, blue sky. "I believe I did. As a matter of fact I believe I did."

We decided on the Starbucks a couple blocks from where I was, along High Street. She told me she'd be there in fifteen minutes. I told her I'd be outside by the door, in a dark blue beret.

"All right," she said, "about fifteen—"

"Hey, Alice?"

"What."

"This is pretty great, huh?"

She didn't say anything.

"Y'know?" I said.

"Okay, bye," she said, and hung up.

I found the off button.

I'll tell you something: you never know. When you get up in the morning, you just never know.

———

I stood outside the Starbucks entrance, enjoying the fact that I wasn't just standing there watching the people go by but was actually waiting for one of them, a young lady named Alice, possibly approaching right here in a yellow dress, merrily swinging her bare brown arms.

She swung on by.

Or hey, what about this one? Long and lanky. Oh, snake woman . . .

She slithered on by.

Or this one here. Oh, that would be nice, to rest my head on those. Rest my weary head . . .

She bounced on by.

The phone rang.

I looked at it in my hand. It rang again. I pressed a button. It rang again. I pressed another one. I heard a man's voice saying, "Hello? Hello?"

I spoke into it. "Yeah. Ray Parisi here."

"Who?"

"Ray Parisi. What do you need?"

"I . . . think I may have dialed the wrong—"

"Who you looking for?"

"Dave. Dave Soderstrom?"

"He's not here right now."

"Oh. I thought this was his cell number."

"Well, he's not here."

"This *is* his cell phone, right?"

"Like I said."

"Well, can I leave a message for him?"

"*Uhhh*, negative."

"Who *is* this?"

"Already told you. Now, look. I don't want to be rude but I'm meeting someone here, a young lady, okay? And she's, well, she's pretty special, put it that way, all right? Enough said?"

"I still don't quite understand . . ."

"Hey," I told him, "don't even try. It's all a mystery, the whole journey, the whole—wait a second, hold on."

Dave was marching up.

I stepped backwards, holding out the phone: "It's for you."

He snatched it out of my hand and spoke into it: "Hang on." Then he told me, "C'mere, you. C'mere."

But I was in a hurry and ran off. I wanted to get back to my garret. I had a fresh idea for my monster series. I would call it, simply, *Alice*.

No Place Like Home

Arnie wondered about Dorothy. She seemed way too big to be wandering around the barnyard in a party dress and pigtails, singing to her little dog about rainbows. Shouldn't she have been helping out? She was bigger than Auntie Em.

There was a pink-faced, Dorothy-sized girl in the neighborhood named Gloria who *also* wore pigtails and party dresses, plus a lot of messy lipstick, and when the older boys shouted, "*Hey, Gloria, show us your panties,*" she would stop her bike and lift up her dress with a horrible smile.

Dorothy didn't seem *that* far gone, but like Gloria, she didn't seem to have any friends—except of course for Toto, and when Miss Gulch took him away in her picnic basket Dorothy didn't just cry, she threw herself across her bed and *sobbed*.

Arnie saw Gloria crying like that once, pedaling hard down the sidewalk, bawling away at the blue sky. Somebody must have done something to her, something bad. He felt sorry.

He felt a little sorry for *Dorothy* when she got locked out of the storm cellar, the cyclone closing in. Auntie Em had called out her name a few times but gave up pretty easily, it seemed. And when Dorothy stomped on the cellar door with her heel, they *had* to have heard. Maybe Auntie Em and Uncle Henry figured this was a good way of getting rid of her. After all, they weren't her real parents, and she didn't contribute anything to the farm, and probably ate as much as three little girls.

Gloria was always gobbling Hostess cream-filled cupcakes. She carried them around in the wire basket on the front of her bike. Sometimes she would pull up by the backstop in the park and eat cupcakes while she watched Arnie and his friends playing ball. He tried not to look, the way she always got cream and crumbs all over her face. After an inning or two she would finally wave and yell, "*Byyye,*" no one replying, and pedal off.

But Dorothy changes. She grows up a little. In fact a lot. It begins with the ruby slippers. Looking down at them on her feet, she goes up on her toes and does a graceful little turn, like a young lady. Then she actually starts being useful. She helps the Scarecrow down from his pole and keeps him on his feet, squirts oil on the Tin Man to get *him* going, and scolds the Cowardly Lion for scaring little Toto. "Shame on you," she tells him.

Gloria scolded Arnie once.

The way it happened, he was walking home from the park one afternoon, just walking along with his bat and glove, then all of a sudden Gloria came bicycling around the corner. "Hi, Arnie!" she shouted, and as she pedaled by and continued on down the sidewalk she cried out, "Bye, Arnie! *Byyye!*" He walked home horrified: Gloria never used anyone's name, she didn't *know* anyone's name, but somehow she knew his, which meant he was in her mind, which made him feel sick deep inside. After that, he started crossing the street whenever he saw her coming, pretending not to see her.

"Hi, Arnie!"

Pretending not to hear.

"Bye, Arnie!"

He had a dream one night in which Gloria was also Dorothy, also the Wicked Witch, wearing ruby slippers as she pedaled her bike across the sky, able to spell, looping out *Hi Arnie* in white smoke for all to see, smiling her lipsticky smile up there.

Then one Saturday morning she was waiting for him. He was coming out of Dorbern's Bakery with a loaf of raisin bread his mom had sent him after, and there she was, straddling her bike and smiling. "Hi, Arnie! Wanna see my panties?"

"No!"

She stopped smiling as if he had slapped her.

Then he told her, slowly so she would understand: "Leave. Me. Alone."

Gloria started breathing hard. She stretched out a fat red arm and pointed at his face. "You're not nice, Arnie." Then she pedaled off, bawling out, *"You're not nice!"*

He gave a shrug to show how little he cared what Gloria thought. Walking home he ate a slice of raisin bread to further show himself, though he had some trouble swallowing.

Dorothy ends up scolding even the Wizard, telling him, "If you were really great and powerful you'd keep your promises!" And he finally does, sort of. But then she wakes up in her bed back in Kansas and seems really *simple* again. "I'm not going to leave here ever, ever again," she promises Auntie Em, who glances at Uncle Henry.

But maybe Dorothy had the right idea, staying close to home. Gloria's body was discovered one morning under some bushes in a park two towns away, her bicycle lying nearby.

Bob and Todd

A burly man in his midthirties was driving along 95 North out of Boston, humming "Where Have All the Flowers Gone?" A scrawny young man in a poncho and hiking boots was standing in the breakdown lane with his thumb out, a duffel bag upright beside him.

"What have we here?" said the driver, and pulled over.

The young man grabbed the duffel bag by its handle and hurried on over to the car. He stooped down to speak through the partly open passenger-side window. "Thanks for stopping!"

The driver leaned over: "Where you headed?"

"North."

"I'm going as far as the Lewiston exit."

"That's great. Thanks. Appreciate it," said the young man, still standing there.

"You getting in?"

"Just wondering. Why'd you stop?"

"You had your thumb out. Thought you might want a lift."

"Sarcasm. Okay."

"You getting in or not?"

"Just seems a little weird, stopping for some guy in a poncho in the middle of nowhere, see what I'm saying?"

"Right, so the only people you'd get in the car with are the ones who don't stop," the driver said, and laughed. "Good luck with *that*."

"Wait, you're leaving?"

"Been interesting."

"I'll get in."

"Jesus."

After he was in, holding the duffel bag between his legs, the young man once again thanked the driver for stopping. "Appreciate it."

The driver checked the traffic behind him and pulled out. "By the way, you're a very *handsome* young fellow," he said.

"Aw, shit."

The driver laughed. "Kidding. So where you going?"

"Just . . . north."

"Yeah but how far?"

"All the way."

"All the way to where?"

"Just . . . all the way."

"That's quite a distance."

"I'll get there."

"You realize, if you do go all the way you'll end up at that same spot along the road back there."

"The Earth is round, I know."

"So let me guess. You've had all you can take and now you're getting the hell out."

"Something like that."

"Turning your back on civilization."

"You could say."

"Maybe go live with the Indians."

"Possibly."

"Adopt the ways of the red man."

"Why not?"

"I wonder what name they'll give you. They do that, you know."

"Fed-Up."

"That's a good one. I like that."

They were quiet for a minute. Then the driver said, "Now *me*, I sell athletic shoes, what you would call 'sneakers.' That's what I'm doing up here, peddling my company's product to outlets in the area. Know what your Indian friends would call *me*? Sells-Athletic-Shoes. By the way, if you're interested, I've got a bunch of samples in the trunk, along with my wife's body."

The young man looked at him.

"But I'm gonna confess something to you now," the driver went on. "Just between you and me, I hate athletic shoes. I hate the way they look on people, especially on adults, on so-called grown-ups. In fact, you know what's wrong with this country? Too many silly-assed people bopping around in sneakers. Nobody's *serious* anymore. Not like you. You're serious. I can tell by your footwear. Hiking boots. Those are serious."

"You mentioned . . ."

"Yeah?"

"Your wife's body?"

"Did I? Nice body—very nice, in fact. No problem *there*, believe me."

"But?"

"Nice butt, yes. Very nice. Why the sudden interest in my wife's body?"

"You said . . . anyway I *thought* you said . . . it's in the trunk."

"My wife's body is in the trunk?"

"Along with your samples."

"I actually said that?"

"I could be wrong."

"Oh, I'm sure you are."

"I was out there for a couple hours, in that sun . . ."

"That'll do it."

The young man gave a laugh. "I really thought you said your wife's body was in the trunk."

"Well," said the driver, "if I did say that, I apologize. I certainly didn't mean to. What do you say we just forget about it, leave the whole thing behind us." He gave a chuckle. "Which is where it is anyway."

Laughing along, the young man said, "I know you're only pulling my leg."

"Well of *course* I'm pulling your leg, what do you think? You think if I shot my wife and stuck her in the trunk I would *tell* you about it? Even accidentally? Come on, use your head. That would mean I'd have to shoot *you* as well, stick *you* in the trunk."

"I know you're only trying to scare me."

"That's all. That's all I'm trying to do. Don't be scared."

"I'm not. If I was scared, that would mean I believed you, which I don't, so I'm not. Scared."

"Well, fine. Can we move on now, please? Let's talk about your future, boldly going where no one has gone before—except, you see, that's just it, there *isn't* any place where no one's gone before, not on *this* fucking planet anyway." He shook his head. "Just once, just *once* I would like to get really and truly totally *lost*, you know? Just once be able to cry out, 'Where the fuck *am* I?' And for an answer? Only an echo: 'Fuck *am* I, fuck *am* I . . .' See what I'm saying?"

"Sir, I was wondering, could I . . . possibly . . ."

"Pee in a cup?"

". . . get out for a minute? Just wanna stretch my legs a little."

"Just wanna *bolt*, you mean. Don't try and kid a kidder: you're still thinking about Betty, aren't ya."

"Was that her name?"

"I thought we had moved on." He sighed. "All right. Look. You want me to pull over and open the trunk and show you? Would that help?"

"It would. Yes. Go ahead, pull over. Stop the car."

"Well, I'm sorry, but you know what? I'm not gonna do that, and I'll tell you why. Because if you don't trust me any more than that, you have no business being with me in the first place."

"You're right. I agree, sir. Completely."

"All right, then."

"So go ahead. Pull over. I'll get out."

"Oh, now . . ."

"No, really. Go ahead. Please?"

"Don't start getting all—"

"Please, sir? Let me out?"

"Will you *listen* to yourself? My *God*. And you want to go live with the Indians? You know what they would call you? Scaredy-Cat. *That's* the name they'd give you. Mine's Bob, by the way. What's yours?"

The young man continued sitting there staring rigidly ahead.

"Let's try that again. *My* name is Bob. What is yours?"

In a weak voice: "Todd."

"Sorry, didn't catch that."

A little louder: "Todd."

"Todd? Is that what you said? 'Todd'?"

"Yes."

Bob gave a laugh. "That's really your name? *Todd?*"

Todd looked at him. "What's wrong with that?"

"Just strikes me kind of funny: Sitting Bull, Crazy Horse, Geronimo . . . and Todd." He laughed harder.

"Yeah well, what about 'Bob'?"

He stopped laughing.

Todd spoke rapidly, "I'm sorry, I didn't mean that, Bob's a good name, a serious name."

"As in what, Bob and Ray? Bob Newhart? Bob Hope? Clowns, Todd."

Todd said quietly, "I'm sorry."

"Let's face it, we've both got less than fully serious names. Bob and Todd: now *there's* a couple of light-weights—although, of course, *my* name is actually Robert, which is *somewhat* serious. But what the hell is 'Todd' short for?"

"Theodore?"

"You're thinking of Ted, like Theodore Roosevelt. His wife used to call him Teddy. 'Oh, Teddy,' she used to say, 'you *do* carry a big stick.' But with his clothes on, in the Oval Office, he was Theodore. Ever been to Mount Rushmore? You might *get* there in your travels. If you do, take a good long look at those faces up there. Those were serious men. I guarantee you, those men did not wear sneakers. And I know what you're thinking."

"No. I wasn't. Honest."

"But maybe it's not too late, you know? For either of us. After all, we're both wearing serious footwear. You've got your boots, and look at me, what *I'm* wearing: wing tips. Classic. Traditional. Serious." He looked at Todd. "*Deadly* serious."

"This looks like a real good spot, right along here. Thanks again." He gave a laugh. "Every little bit helps. Really appreciate it. If you could just pull over, sir. Right here would be . . . would be . . ."

"Know who used to wear wing tips?"

Todd sat there looking longingly out his window at the side of the road.

"I asked you a question, Todd. Do you know who used to wear wing tips? Always? On all occasions?"

"No."

"Take a guess."

"Theodore Roosevelt?"

"My *father* wore wing tips. My old man. Now *there* was a serious person. There was a man who believed in the basic fundamental seriousness of life. He used to say to me, 'Robert?'—he always called me Robert, never Bob. In fact, *no one* ever called me Bob, not even my friends, not even my enemies. It was always Robert. It wasn't Bob until I got married. That's when all this Bob business began. And you know who started it? So that *everyone* calls me Bob now? *Thinks* of me as Bob? Even myself? You know who started all this Bob shit?"

Todd looked over at him slowly. "Betty?"

Bob was quiet for a moment. Then: "My father would put his hand on my shoulder, his massive hand on my little shoulder. 'Robert?' he would say, closing his hand like a fucking vise: 'Life . . . is no . . . joke.'"

The road curved eastward, putting the sun in their eyes. Bob lowered his visor and Todd did the same.

Bob went on, "My father died from a stroke one afternoon sitting on the couch watching television. Know what he was watching, Todd? Do you know what he was sitting there in front of, with his eyes still open? Take a guess. Go ahead."

"The market report?"

"Bob Barker. *The Price Is Right.*"

Todd said quietly, "I'm sorry."

"Sorry. You're always sorry. You're about the sorriest motherfucker I ever met, you know that? And don't say you're sorry."

They were quiet.

"No, listen," Bob said wearily, "I'm the one who should be sorry, snapping at you like that. It's just . . . well, I feel like you've got real possibilities, Todd. The makings of a serious person. It just has to be drawn out, that's all. Or dragged out."

"Could we listen to the radio for a while, you think?"

"Hey, Todd, look at that old red barn out there, will ya? See it out there? Isn't that a beautiful thing? Isn't it?"

"Yes."

"I can picture an old, gaunt-looking farmer going out to that barn at four thirty in the morning to milk the cows, can't you?"

"I guess."

"Meanwhile his wife is in the kitchen fixing breakfast, a quiet dignified woman named Sarah." He shook his head. "Take a real good look at that barn, Todd, because the next time you see it? The next time around? I guarantee, that old red barn will be an upscale furniture and gift shop. And you know what they'll call it? The sons-a-bitches, you know what they'll call that goddamn furniture and gift shop? 'The Old Red Barn.'"

They drove along.

Todd asked again if they could listen to the radio.

"Nah. You want some music? Here you go. Remember this one?" He sang, "*Where have all the flowers gone, long time pa-assing* . . . Sing along, Todd, come on. *Where have all the flowers gone, long time ago* . . ."

Todd wasn't singing.

Bob looked at him. "Aw, Jesus, you're not *crying*, are you?"

Todd turned away, to his window.

"Listen, do me a favor," Bob said. "I got a pack of Camel Filters in the glove box. Get 'em for me, will you? Can you do that for me, please?"

Todd opened the glove box, cried "*Ahh!*" and slammed it shut.

"What's the matter? You okay?"

Todd sat there staring straight ahead, breathing fast and shallow.

"Oh, hey, listen," said Bob, "I'm sorry, I forgot that was in there. Now, don't start getting all worked up the way you do. I know what you're thinking: the murder weapon. Right? Tell the truth, Todd. Isn't that what you're thinking?"

Todd nodded.

Bob said to him quietly, seriously, "You know what this is, Todd, don't you? This is what your Indian friends would call a moment of truth."

"Please let me out? Please, Bob? *Robert* I mean."

"Now, listen to me, Todd. Listen carefully. Let's say you're right. Let's say I really did kill my wife, with that very gun. Shot her three times, right through her silly fucking heart, then cut her up into a dozen pieces, each in its own plastic bag, put all twelve bags into separate shoe boxes, and placed them in the trunk with all the other shoe boxes. Let's say I'm that kind of a guy. That would put you in serious jeopardy right now, wouldn't it." He waited. "Todd? Wouldn't it?"

"Yes."

"Okay, but here's the thing. That leaves three more bullets in the gun, Todd. For either one of us."

"I promise, I swear to God I won't ever—"

"Tell anyone?"

"I swear to *God*."

"Todd, you're missing the point. Stay focused. This is important."

"I want to go home."

"I thought you were fed up. Thought you were going *allll* the way."

"That was just . . . I was only . . ."

"Pretending. I know. But listen to me. Remember what I said earlier? About turning things around? About getting serious? Even with a name like Todd? Well, here it is, buddy. Here's your chance. Don't blow it."

"Can't we just . . . can't we just . . . ?"

"Look. I know you're scared. Believe me, I know all about it. Right now you've got this cold, hollow spot in the pit of your tummy and your heart is beating like a little bunny rabbit's—but *think* about it, Todd. You're in the driver's seat—so to speak. Just open the glove box, grab the gun and shoot me, steer the car into the breakdown lane, apply the brakes, and put it in park, simple as that. What is it Nike says? 'Just *do* it.'"

"Please? Can't we just—"

"Shut up. Now listen to me, you fucking dweeb, I'm going to kill you, do you realize that? I'm gonna shoot you dead with that gun unless you stop me." He began slowly leaning over in front of Todd, keeping one hand on the wheel, eyes on the road. "Here I am, Todd," he said in a singsong, "reaching for the glove box . . ."

Todd sat there covering his face, rocking.

"Reaching for the gun," Bob sang, "so I can shoot you, then stuff you in the trunk with Betty . . ."

"Can't we just listen to the radio?"

Bob sat up straight again. He pulled off into the breakdown lane and came to a stop. "Get out of my car," he said quietly, staring straight ahead.

Todd got out very quickly with his duffel bag and closed the door.

The car pulled away.

Todd watched it becoming just another car among all the others. Then, at a large enough break in the traffic both ways, he hurried all the way across, set down his duffel bag, and held out his thumb.

Made for Each Other

"Do you like my outfit, Ken?"

Barbie was wearing a yellow chiffon evening dress with lavender heels, long white gloves, and a sun hat.

"You look nice."

"Oh, Ken, that's so sweet."

"What about *my* outfit?" he asked, dressed for a safari.

"You look handsome in a helmet."

"Thanks. Go for a walk?"

"I would *love* to."

They hopped along the carpet together.

"What nice weather we're having," Barbie remarked. "Don't you think?"

"Uh-*huh*."

Marcia told Randy, "No, have him say, 'It's *always* nice when *you're* around.'"

"All right. Say again about the weather."

"What nice weather we're having, don't you think?"

"It's *always* nice when *you're* around."

"Oh, Ken, that's so sweet."

"Care to dance?"

"I would *love* to."

They hopped in place, facing each other, tilting this way and that, Marcia humming a bouncy tune.

"You're a good dancer, Barbie."

"Oh, Ken, that's so sweet."

"You say that a lot."

Barbie stopped dancing. "So? What's wrong with that?"

"Nothing. Don't get mad."

"Stop dancing, Ken."

He stopped.

Barbie hopped up closer to him. "Will you tell me something, please?"

"What."

"Do you love me or not?"

Ken turned this way and that.

"Well?" she said.

"*Oh no, a tornado!*" he cried, and was thrown to the ceiling. He landed on his back and lay there moaning.

"I asked you a question, Ken."

"I think my back is broken."

"Stop changing the subject. Do you love me or not?"

Ken managed to get to his feet. He looked at her. "Not," he said.

Barbie stood there a moment. Then she said, "Oh . . . *Ken*," and threw herself down on the carpet.

Ken leaned over her. "Barbie, listen . . ."

"You broke . . . my . . . *heart*," she said through her tears.

"No, listen, you're a doll, Barbie. You're a *doll*, okay?"

Barbie stood up, sniffling. "Oh, Ken, that's so sweet."

"No, I mean you're a *doll*, you're made out of plastic, and so am I. We're both just a couple of stupid little—"

Marcia swung Barbie at Ken so hard he flew out of Randy's hand.

Randy looked at Marcia, who was kneeling there holding up Barbie like a weapon.

"You can't do that, Randy."

He carefully reached behind and picked up Ken, keeping an eye on Marcia, who said again, slowly shaking her head, "You can't do that."

Randy held up *Ken* like a weapon. "Wanna bet?"

They knelt there, eyes locked.

Randy faked as if to swing, Marcia flinching. He smiled. She swung and caught him right across the smile with Barbie's head. He cried out, dropping Ken, and put his hand to his mouth: blood. He showed Marcia his hand.

"Sorry. Would you hand me her hat please? It's right there by your knee."

Randy carefully dabbed a fleck of blood onto Ken's mouth.

"What're you *doing*?"

He set Ken on his feet. "You broke my lip, Barbie."

"Well, *you* broke my *heart*," Barbie replied, Marcia holding her upright on the floor again.

Ken began hopping slowly toward her. "It's bleeding bad."

"So is my heart, Ken."

He kept coming. "I hate you."

"You don't mean that, I know you don't."

"Yes I do. I hate everything about you."

"Ken . . ."

"The way you talk, the way you dress, the way you dance. You. Make. Me. *Sick*."

"Ken, I've never *seen* you like this. You're scaring me."

"I'm going to kill you, Barbie. I'm going to yank your stupid little head off. What do you think of that?"

"Stay away from me."

He kept coming.

Marcia told Randy, "Make him stop."

"I'm *trying* to. Honest. I can't. He's alive!"

"Enough, Randy. Enough."

"Tell *him*."

"Ken, stop," Barbie told him.

He kept coming.

"You're a *doll*," she told him.

"I'm a what?"

"A doll, Ken."

He stood there, tilting to one side. "Oh, Barbie, that's so sweet."

Marcia sat back on her heels and looked at Randy.

"What," he said.

"I hate you."

"No, don't. Come on. Look what you did to my lip."

"Look what you did to *them*!"

"What'd I do?"

"Nothing, you just ruined everything, that's all, the whole romance, it's over!" She flung Barbie across the room, then covered her face and cried.

"Don't, will you? Marcia? I'm sorry. Please?"

She kept on.

"I was jealous," he told her, "Okay? Okay?"

Marcia slid her hands from her wet face and looked at him.

He looked down at the carpet.

"You were jealous?" Marcia said. "Of Ken?"

He shrugged.

"You don't have to answer this, Randy, okay? But are you in love with Barbie?"

He looked at Marcia. "*No.*"

"So then . . . you mean . . . ?"

He looked down again.

"Oh," she said, nodding slowly. "*Hmm,*" she said. "I see."

He looked at her. "Can I say something? Promise you won't laugh?"

Marcia promised.

He said to her, "It's always nice when *you're* around."

Marcia burst out laughing.

Randy got up and ran from the room. She listened for the back door to open, then close. *Poor Randy,* she thought. *I shouldn't have laughed at him, that wasn't nice. Or whacked him quite so hard.*

She looked over at Ken. He was lying on his back, in his safari outfit. There was blood on his mouth, but *he* wasn't being a baby about it: gazing straight up, smiling bravely.

THE MUMMY

I still haven't cried. That's not good.

It's been snowing since this morning. I've closed the blinds, wrapped myself in an afghan, and hunkered down on the floor in front of the television. Boris Karloff is wearing a fez and a long, narrow robe. He doesn't move his arms when he walks or allow anyone to touch him. When the professor offers his hand to shake, he stands there looking at it.

I called the office earlier and told Rhonda I wouldn't be in, that I have a "stomach issue." The truth is, I'm staying home waiting to cry.

Last night Jerry said to me, "Allen, I've met someone."

I didn't know what he meant. I said, "Oh? Who?"

"His name is Brian."

We were doing the dishes. He was washing, I was drying.

"Brian," I said.

"Yes," he said, and explained what he meant.

Then I did have a stomach issue. I gave him back the plate he had just handed me, hurried to the bathroom, and threw up in the toilet.

Jerry stood in the doorway. "Allen, I am so . . . so . . ."

I stepped over to the door and closed it in his face, locked it, and returned to the toilet. I was honestly wishing I could throw up my heart along with the mac and cheese we'd eaten twenty minutes earlier. When I was through I washed up at the sink. Then I held on to it with both hands, head bowed, and waited for the salty waters to come pouring forth.

I'm still waiting. Jerry's been gone since last night and I've yet to shed a single fucking tear. That's not good. That's not healthy.

The movie shows a close-up of Boris Karloff staring into the camera with his mesmerizing eyes.

Oh, go away, you silly man.

Know who would love this movie? Jerry. He would have taken this movie very seriously. Boris Karloff returning from the dead to search for his reincarnated girlfriend—Jerry would have found that incredibly romantic: *Think of it, Allen, his love has lasted through thousands of years.*

And yours lasted less than three, you shit.

You *shit*.

The truth is, Jerry was a lot of talk. I'm not saying he was insincere. I'm sure he meant every loving thing he ever said to me, just as I'm sure he means every loving thing he's telling this Brian person now.

Boris Karloff finally meets Helen. She's the one. And when he gets her in an ancient Egyptian eye-lock, she recalls in a murky way what they had together twenty-seven hundred years ago. I do a quick calculation: if each of her incarnations lasted an average of seventy years, she's been through something like forty other lives since she and Boris were an item.

I'm a cost accountant for Whitney Imports.

And yet he still reaches her, through all those other lives, Jerry would be saying. *That's how strong their love was, Allen. That's how powerful.*

And I'd be saying, *Jerry, the man wants to turn her into a living mummy like himself—does that sound to you like a healthy relationship?*

He would tell me I was absolutely hopeless.

But here's the thing: we'd be sitting there together on the couch holding hands.

The girl, Helen, has met a fellow from *this* life, handsome, earnest Frank with a strong chin. I don't like him. I'm sure he's absolutely right for her, but I find myself pulling more and more for Boris Karloff. Don't get me wrong, I think his obsession over this woman, his inability to let go after twenty-seven hundred years, and his horrible intentions for her all add up to a very sick individual. But who ever said love was supposed to be healthy?

Actually, *I* did.

Jerry was forever making fun of what a level-headed, unromantic person I am. But it never hurt, because I knew he understood—or I *thought* he understood—that *one* of us had to keep room in his soul for things like Tuesday being trash day.

The movie ends with Frank and Helen in each other's arms, Boris Karloff having turned into a pile of twenty-seven-hundred-year-old dust on the floor. I turn it off. I get up and go to the window and raise the blinds. It's snowing harder now, coming down in big, crisscrossing flakes. I hope it keeps up. I hope it snows and snows until everything finally stops, utterly still, utterly mummified.

But the fucking plows are out. I can hear them.

Tomorrow morning I'll put out the garbage, then drive to work along the cleared-off roads, mumble good morning to Rhonda on the way to my desk, everything waiting in tidy piles the way I left it Friday, with no idea.

I let my forehead rest against the cold window.

I'll just go on, that's all. After a few months, three or four, it will stop hurting, or anyway *begin* to stop. Another month or so after that and I'll be fine, I'll stop loving him and be fine. And that's the saddest thing of all: I'll be fine.

Ah, here they come, the tears, here they are.

A Matter of Character

"*Talk to me, talk to me . . .*"

I don't know what she wants to hear.

"*Talk to me . . .*"

We're having sex but we just met tonight.

"*Talk to me, talk to me . . .*"

I whisper in her ear, "How 'bout those Cubbies?"

She shoves me off her.

I tell her I'm sorry. I tell her I didn't know what to say. I tell her the Cubs are only two games out of first.

She calls me a fucking idiot, gets dressed, and leaves.

I heat up some soup, Campbell's chicken noodle.

Eating it over the sink, I stare at the moon above the 7-Eleven. That was stupid, *How 'bout those Cubbies.* I don't even care about the Cubs. In fact I wish they would go back to losing. I used to catch a game now and then—my apartment's not far—and it was nice there, Wrigley Field is such a pretty place. I'd buy a hot dog. It was like being at a huge picnic. But now everyone's on their feet screaming for them to win and it's not as pleasant.

I wash the pan and spoon.

I'm thinking about going back to the bar—it's not even ten yet—and trying again. I get laid fairly regular, tall and handsome as I am. This girl tonight, Doreen I think her name was, told me I kind of look a little bit like Peter Fonda, from that hippie movie last year, *Easy Rider*. If you haven't seen it, don't bother. There's no *plot* going on. Anyway, just to be polite I told this Doreen she kind of looked like Karen Black, Peter Fonda's girl in the movie. Actually, she looked more like the president's wife, but I didn't tell her—the way she was dressed, she probably wanted to look a lot sexier than that.

But I like Pat Nixon. She seems brave, the way she always keeps her smile and good posture. I don't know about her husband, he seems kind of conniving—but he isn't Adolf Hitler like the hippies would have you think. He's just trying to bring a little order into all this. Like my dad says, this country *needs* someone to crack the whip a little.

Ever see Nixon's golf swing, though? Yikes. Dad says if he'd seen that swing before the election he never would have voted. Dad's very big on golf.

He's also very big on America. You should see the flag on his front porch, the size of it. He earned a medal over in Korea and thinks I belong in Vietnam, but they wouldn't take me. Bad knees, they said. I was glad. They've probably got some humongous insects over there. I hate bugs. That's the reason I always eat over the sink and clean up right afterwards.

Cockroaches, that's all I need.

They say if there was a nuclear war and the whole planet was blown to smithereens the only survivors would be cockroaches, radioactivity being like mother's milk to those fuckers. They'd be the size of cars. Can you imagine?

Which is why it's so important that we hold the line in Vietnam. The hippies all want us to leave, but as soon as we do the whole place will go Communist, and *then* what?

I'm not real sure. To be honest, I don't know that much about it. I just know I don't like hippies, especially the way they dance.

They have this dance floor at the bar and I enjoy going out there with a girl, bad knees and all, and doing an actual particular *dance* together, the funky chicken or the swim or even the twist. But these hippies, they just go out there and start doing whatever, mostly just flinging themselves around. That shouldn't be allowed, especially with all the fringes and beads and crap they all wear. Somebody's going to lose an eye.

I decide to call it a night. I have to get up early tomorrow. So I get in my pajama bottoms and watch some TV. I've got this little black-and-white on the floor by the couch and sometimes I like to just sprawl there and stare at whatever's on.

Star Trek is just starting.

I think I'd be happy on that starship. They'd probably have me waiting tables, same as down here, but I'd be very happy doing my part along with the rest of the crew, meanwhile flying at warp speed farther and farther away.

After I go to bed I have this dream again about my mom. She died three years ago, breast cancer, slow and awful, and I keep having this dream where I'm eight years old or so, standing in the middle of the kitchen in my seersucker pajamas. She's sitting at the table in her housecoat flipping through a magazine, *Good Housekeeping*, smoking a Lucky Strike, eating potato chips with a bottle of Pepsi. There's dirty dishes in the sink, bugs crawling around on them. Mom looks at me and smiles. "C'mere, Benny." She jabs out her cigarette in the loaded ashtray and holds out her arms. "C'mere and give Mommy a hug." I keep standing there. And that's it, the whole dream.

The reason I have to get up early is to go golfing with my dad. We go every other week, early spring to late fall. Trouble is, I don't go any other time—to be honest, I'm not that fond of the game—so I stay pretty lousy, especially compared to him. You should see his trophy case from all the amateur tournaments he's won. He's also got three golf balls with a different date written on each, for the three different holes-in-one he's had. The thing he really cherishes, though, is this book signed by Arnold Palmer:

> *To Jim,*
> *Best wishes!*
> *—Arnold Palmer*

Dad loves Arnold Palmer. He wears sweaters just like him—in fact they're called Arnold Palmer sweaters. He's got about a dozen, in every color. He's wearing his light blue one this morning. I'm in my mirrored sunglasses and good pants—he gets pissed off if I show up in jeans. I'm also wearing one of the many golf shirts he's given me, a bright yellow one to go with this bright, sunny morning. I always try to seem glad to be here, like this is terrific, out here golfing with my old man.

He doesn't look at all like Arnold Palmer, by the way, even in the sweaters. He looks more like the channel 7 newscaster Fahey Flynn, only a lot heavier and not as twinkly-eyed, not nearly.

But Jesus, can he ever golf.

It disappoints him a lot, how lousy I am. He thinks it has to do mostly with character. He says golf is only 35 percent skill, which he says I've got, and the rest is character, which he says I lack.

He starts in on that shit this morning.

We're on the third tee, waiting on this pokey four-some ahead of us. He's one under par and I'm already five over. He refuses to believe I'm that bad: "You have an excellent swing, Ben," he's telling me. "A little bit flat but so is Arnie's, and I don't think *he's* done too badly with it. But here's what else he's got: a fierce determination to win—in whatever he does, not just golf."

"Dad . . ."

"A man who's able to look straight down the fairway of life, straight down to where he wants to be, and then *go* there. He even flies his own plane, did you know that?"

I did.

It bothers Dad that I'm working as a waiter in a Mexican restaurant, that I'm twenty-two years old waiting tables at the Silver Sombrero, whereas *he* at my age was already setting up his own company: Chalmers Home Insulation, call and ask for Jim.

"The road to success is always under construction, Ben," he reminds me now, quoting Arnie, meaning it's not too late to change my pointless life.

"Jesus, Dad," I blurt, "can't we just *play* for once?"

So that's it. He goes totally stone-faced and silent.

Which is fine, you know? Fine with me.

The foursome is on the green by now, so I go ahead and tee up my ball, get in my stance, don't even hesitate, just swing. And Jesus, will you look at that. It takes off in a low line drive but then it starts rising, rising, and then it just *sits* up there a while enjoying the view before beginning its descent, and when it finally lands it goes leaping straight ahead, takes a bunch of smaller and smaller bounces, then rolls another ten yards before coming to a stop, dead center of the fairway, 250 yards out there at least, at *least.*

Dad doesn't say a word. Absolutely the best drive I ever made in my entire life and he's got nothing to say.

Me neither. I pick up my tee.

I hate this. I really do.

He tees up, and as he stands over the ball I can tell what he wants to do with it, fucking crush it, show me how a man of *character* hits the ball, send it fifty yards beyond mine, and he ends up doing something rare for him: he overswings, hooking it badly, off into the trees.

I feel like saying, *See what happened here, Dad? You got angry, you let it affect your swing, and look at the result.* But all I say is "Ah, gee," like I feel bad for him.

We pick up our bags in silence, hoist them onto our shoulders, and while *he* goes off into the jungle I go for a stroll down the middle of the fairway. We never use a cart, even the kind you pull around by hand, Dad being very old-school. You carry your clubs on your shoulder. Those clubs are your friends, he says, and you want to stay close to your friends.

When I finally arrive at my ball, I set down my rattling bag and wait to see Dad's shot from off in the wilds. I don't know what he uses but he drills it low, threading the trees and reaching all the way to the green, in fact rolling to the other side of it and down a slope, where I think there's a sand trap waiting.

"Ah, gee," I whisper, pulling out my four iron. I get in my stance, wiggle my ass, look at the flag rippling in the distance, look at the ball, swing—and there goes *another* fine shot, look at that, fading to the right but not badly, rolling up just a few yards off to the right of the green.

I wait for Dad to holler something, *Well done* or something, before I remember we're not speaking. I watch him trudge on over towards his ball.

I'm beginning to feel a little bit sorry for the guy.

He explodes the ball out of the sand and up onto the green but it rolls past the cup and doesn't stop for another ten yards. He comes up, muttering to himself, and holds the flag for me. I use my wedge and take a short, easy stroke like he's taught me with a shot like this and loft it softly onto the green, rolling off to the right a little, stopping three feet from the hole.

That was pretty, and I know Dad's thinking how pretty, but he just sets down the flag, steps over to his ball and squats behind it, holding the putter up vertically in front of his face and closing one eye. He explained to me once what he's doing when he does that but I forget now. Then he stands over the ball. And you can see, you can really see him gathering back all his calmness and confidence and character, and he taps a beautiful putt, allowing for a long dip in the green, curving towards the hole, curving *around* the hole, then sitting there on the lip, refusing to fall.

Ah, gee.

I wait while he taps it in, takes it out and moves away so I can sink this fucking thing. I've never once beaten Dad on a hole before, and as I stand over the ball, looking at the cup three feet away and tracing an imaginary dotted line back to the ball, I tell myself to tap it firm enough, give it a chance.

I putt.

It heads straight for the hole, then a foot away starts falling off to the left, slides on by, and continues for another three feet, leaving me the same putt coming back. I look straight up at the sky and holler, "*Fuck!*"

Believe it or not, that's the first time I've ever used that word in front of Dad. He has no comment, though, just stands there off to the side waiting with the flag, watching me miss the return three-footer, miss the following *one*-footer, and tap it in for a seven, losing the hole by two strokes.

How's that for character?

————————

We're on the eighth hole, still not speaking. I'm off among the tall grass and the bugs, looking for my ball, swiping around with my six iron, Dad already on the green, waiting. I give up and go to my bag for another ball, my fourth one already. Looking towards the green I see him lying there on his back, one knee raised, which is something he would never do, lie down on the green like that, and I holler out, "*Dad?*"

He doesn't answer, doesn't move.

I drop my club and run over to him. When I get there his face is gray, the eyes a little bit open but not like they're seeing anything, and there isn't any breathing going on. Straddling his fat stomach I sit there pounding the left side of his chest, telling him, "*Talk to me . . . talk to me . . . talk to me . . .*"

Dad's now wearing his dark green Arnold Palmer sweater, along with lipstick and rouge. His putter is in there with him—Uncle Pete's idea—his hands around the grip like he's holding it, but he isn't really. He isn't holding anything anymore.

Standing over him I promise, not out loud: *I'm gonna keep golfing, Dad. I'm gonna get good, make you proud. Get some character too, watch and see. Say hi to Mom.*

Later, Uncle Pete goes up to the podium and talks about what a wonderful older brother Dad was, how he learned so much from him, and not just about home insulation but about life itself, the meaning of life, things like that, Dad always teaching him, always correcting him, always, constantly. Then he talks about Dad's service in Korea and the medal he got, how much he loved his country, the size of the flag he always displayed. And then about golf, all the trophies

Dad won, how he always kept them polished and prominent, first thing you'd see when you walked in the door. He finishes by speaking to the ceiling like he's talking to Dad and says he bets they've got some awfully beautiful golf courses up there: "I'll bet they're really something, Jim, really . . . something," and breaks down crying, Aunt Connie coming up and helping him back to his chair.

Afterwards there's food and drink at Uncle Pete's. People from the company are there, a few from the country club, mostly people I don't recognize. Dad had a lot of friends, or anyway a lot of people he knew. Uncle Pete comes up to me. I'm nursing a can of beer in the corner and he comes over wanting to know what I thought of his speech—his *eulogy*, as he calls it. I tell him I thought it was fine, real good.

"Not too short?"

"Not at all."

"Not too *long*, though, was it?"

"It was just about right, Uncle Pete."

"Afraid I kind of lost it at the end there."

"Yeah, well . . ."

"A good way to finish though, you know? People were touched. They could see it was genuine. Those were real tears, Ben. I loved your dad. He was my *brother*, for Christ sake."

I nod, agreeing.

We stand there looking at the roomful of people eating, drinking, talking, laughing.

"Everyone seems to be holding up pretty well," he says.

I nod, agreeing.

Then he faces me. "Listen, you want those golf trophies? That would be a nice thing to have, wouldn't it? A nice memento?"

"All of 'em?"

He puts his hand on my shoulder. "I think that would be your dad's wish, Ben, don't you?"

"I don't have any *room*, Uncle Pete."

He takes his hand back. "Yeah, well, *I* don't want the damn things."

"What about the country club?"

"I already asked. They don't want 'em either."

"Well, don't just throw them out, okay?"

He stares at me. "Jesus, Ben, what the hell do you think I am? The man was my *brother*, for Christ sake."

I nod, agreeing.

We stand there sipping our beers.

"Maybe I'll bring 'em over to Goodwill," he says. "Donate 'em. That would be nice for somebody, wouldn't it? Some loser? Have a trophy or two? Make him feel good about himself?"

"What about down in the basement?" I ask him. "You have a basement here, right? What about down there?"

"I don't want the goddamn things in the *house*," he shouts, "Okay?"

Everyone looks.

He holds up his beer: "To Jim!"

———

I take the trophies, minus the cabinet. Uncle Pete dumps them all in a big cardboard box, which just fits in one end of my closet. I feel bad keeping them in there like that, but I don't want a bunch of trophies all over the place—that would look show-offy. I end up taking just one of them out, one of the smaller ones, and keeping it on the nightstand by the bed, next to the alarm clock. The little shiny golden guy on the pedestal is just finishing his swing, gazing off into the distance, admiring what a beautiful drive.

"Did you win this?" this girl Abby wants to know, studying the little man, half off the bed, naked, drunk.

"My dad," I tell her.

"So what're *you* doing with it?"

"He's dead."

"Sorry. Hey, guess what. I think the little man's got a boner."

"Leave it, will ya?"

She touches the front of the little pants with the tip of her finger. "He's so *hard*."

"Leave it alone."

She comes back laughing, throwing her long, skinny arm across my chest. "What's-a matter, boobie?"

"Nothing."

"Disrespectful?"

"Little bit."

She sits up all of a sudden. "Aw fuck, I think I'm gonna be . . ."

I point the way towards the bathroom.

She gets up and hurries off.

I move over to the edge of the bed and take a look at the little golfer guy. It was a crease in his pants she was seeing, that's all. Then I notice something I'm surprised I didn't notice before: the face looks so *sad*. Maybe his tee shot *wasn't* so beautiful, maybe he shanked it. Except, he looks a lot sadder than that, like he could almost start crying.

She's throwing up in there now. I hope she's being accurate. I also hope she notices the bottle of Listerine I always keep on the sink.

She comes back feeling all better, the toilet flushing behind her, and she *did* use the Listerine. We start going at it again.

"Hang on a second," I tell her, and roll over to the little golfer guy, turn him towards the wall, and roll back to her. "Okay."

———

She leaves the next morning.

"See ya round," she says.

"You bet," I tell her, still in bed.

I've got the day off and I'm lying there wondering what to do with it. To tell you the truth, I feel like staying in bed. I'm feeling kind of depressed, not sure why. But I made a promise to Dad and get up and get dressed to go golfing. I have a lifetime membership at the country club since last year, from Dad for my birthday. My clubs are there in a locker, waiting.

Those clubs are your friends, Ben.

I take the bus, wearing one of his Arnie sweaters, although it's way too roomy. Uncle Pete gave me the whole collection, except of course the one Dad's wearing.

I end up playing a very decent eighteen holes for me, keeping Dad's advice in mind, keeping my head down, both hands locked and working together, *sweeping* the club back, and when I fuck up, instead of getting mad, trying to figure out what I did wrong. I shoot a

92—which, like I said, for me is very decent. And not only that, I get a birdie, my first ever. This was on a par four and I belted a long, straight drive, but my next shot put me in the rough. I came out very nicely though with a six iron, the ball heading straight for the green, landing in front, bouncing on, and then I lost sight of it. I figured it must have gone over. But when I got there and looked on the other side I couldn't find it. I couldn't find it anywhere. Then, almost like a joke, I went and looked in the hole. You cannot imagine how pretty that ball looked sitting in there.

And you know what hole that was? The eighth, the one where Dad died. Kind of spooky, wouldn't you say?

But that's nothing compared to when I get back to the apartment.

I'm sitting there on the edge of the bed, all worn out. Eighteen holes is a lot of walking, especially with a bag of clubs on your shoulder—but I know Dad would be disappointed to see me using even a pull cart. So anyway I'm sitting there resting up before I go take a shower and I happen to look over at the nightstand and notice the trophy is still facing the wall from last night, which seems disrespectful, so I go over and turn it around. And I know you're not going to believe this, but the sad little golfer guy from last night? He's smiling now.

I get the hell out of there.

———————

I don't come back until late, with an overweight hippie chick in tow. She's wearing a long glass-beaded necklace over one of those tie-dyed psychedelic T-shirts, her hair in two long braids like an Indian maiden, and she definitely *danced* like a hippie, flinging her fat self around like she was having a conniption fit. I did some flinging around out there myself tonight—I didn't feel like doing the fucking twist or *anything* halfway civilized.

Her name is Bridget—or Brenda, I'm not sure. We undress each other, staggering around a little, giggling about it, and get into bed. I don't even look at the little golfer guy, even glance at him. Not interested. She opens her chubby legs and I climb inside. Then everything is fine.

Afterwards I roll off her and over to the edge of the bed, to the nightstand, to the trophy, to the little man, just curious.

I give a groan.

"What's the matter?" she says.

"This is way too fucking weird," I say.

She sits up. "What is?"

I hold up the trophy. "Look at this."

"Yeah? So? Congratulations."

I hand it to her. "Look at the little man, at his face."

She looks. "What about it?"

I tell her about earlier today, how happy he looked, all smiles. "I'd been out *golfing*, right? But *now* look at him."

"I am. What'm I suppose to see?"

"How *sad* he is again, like he's gonna start crying."

She hands him back, shaking her head: "Man, you must be *on* something. Are you?"

I check the face again. "For fuck sake, the guy is practically—"

"Please stop? You're freaking me out, okay?"

"Well I'm sorry but we're talking here about my *father*, y'know? My dead father. Where you going?"

"I forgot, I'm supposed to be somewhere," she says, getting up.

"Aw, come on, don't go."

"I completely forgot." She's grabbing her clothes from the floor and yanking them on as fast as she can, scared of me.

I tell her, "Stay, come on. Will you? I don't feel like being alone, okay? I'm not dangerous, Brenda. Honest."

"It's Bridget," she says, dressed now. "And I mean this sincerely: you need help, my friend."

"So stay and help."

"*Professional* help," she explains, and wishes me luck.

After she's gone I sit there on the edge of the bed, still holding the trophy, thinking maybe she's right. Maybe what I should do is just check myself *in* somewhere, you know? Watch *Days of Our Lives* in my pajamas, along with the others.

—*Insanity's a cop-out, Ben.*

The tiny face looks angry now.

—*Show some character, for God sakes.*

I decide to.

I get up and take him to the closet, dump him in the box with the others and close the door. Heading back, I *think* I hear him holler "*Attaboy*," but I'm not sure. I mean, we're talking here about a fucking golf trophy.

————

I don't have to be at work the next morning until eleven, so I'm out there teeing off by eight, not too badly hung over. I don't bother with a scorecard. It's a nice morning and I just want to play a few holes, hit the ball around. There's this feeling when you meet it just right, this clean, sweet feeling. That's all I'm after.

I use a pull cart.

Nancy Drew and the Case of the Missing Slipper

CHAPTER I: A STARTLING DISCOVERY

"Ten, nine, eight, seven, six, five, four . . ."

The elderly, white-haired sleuth stood in front of the microwave in her quilted housecoat, heating a bowl of canned prunes for thirty seconds, counting out loud the final ten.

". . . three, two, *one*."

The boxy apparatus gave a cheerful *ding*, as she knew it would.

After yanking open the small door she reached in with both hands, lifted out the bowl, and set it on the countertop—quickly, for it was hot. She then stepped back to the microwave, shut the door, and returned to the prunes. Once again taking up the bowl—which had already cooled off enough by now—she carried it carefully toward the living room, where, thinking ahead, she had already set up a small folding table in front of the couch, with a spoon and paper napkin.

Her intention was to eat the prunes while watching the Weather Channel.

But as she was leaving the kitchen she noticed something curious. The tile floor felt quite cool under the sole of her right foot but not cool at all under the left one. She stopped walking and looked down at her feet.

Her right slipper was missing!

CHAPTER II: A CURIOUS CLUE

Nancy immediately turned around and, still holding the bowl of prunes, began retracing her steps, carefully searching the floor for any sign of the missing slipper.

She had a strong suspicion who was behind this: her long-deceased father, the famous attorney Carson Drew. He frequently challenged her from beyond the grave, setting up mysteries designed to keep her sleuthing skills in A1 condition. The other day he hid her hairbrush.

She still hadn't solved *that* case.

Once again Nancy set the bowl of prunes on the countertop, then returned to the microwave, where she hesitated for just a moment, then with both hands pulled open the little door.

No slipper.

Nancy continued standing there, staring for a long while at a soup stain on the back wall of the microwave. The shape of the stain was very intriguing. The longer she stared the more she realized what a striking resemblance it bore to a Chinese dragon. Could that be a clue?

Chinese dragon . . . Chinese New Year . . . fire-crackers . . . crackers . . . crumbs . . .

"Of course!" she said to herself.

CHAPTER III: A PAINFUL MEMORY

Nancy closed the microwave door and began making her way toward the yellow plastic garbage container at the other end of the kitchen. Earlier, when she had swept the floor after spilling some crumbs from her toast and raspberry jam, her father must have somehow caused her right slipper to detach itself from her foot. She then must have unwittingly swept the slipper into the dustpan along with the crumbs and tossed it in the garbage!

She smiled to herself, picturing her handsome father, the way he would so often shake his head, telling her, "Nancy, you're amazing!"

In fact, *everyone* said so.

She stopped walking.

Everyone, that is, except her ex-beau Ned Nickerson.

Oh, he agreed she was an amazing, brilliant *sleuth*. But in bed? Not so amazing, not so brilliant. "A cold fish," that was what he had called her. Was there anything in the world less appealing than a cold—presumably dead—fish? He didn't deny that she was very attractive: her titian hair, her ripe little mouth, her creamy skin, her perky breasts. "But you're stuck in *here*," he told her, tapping her forehead with a meaty finger. After the breakup, Nancy's father tried to comfort her, acknowledging that Ned was indeed a fine young man. "But let's face it," he added, "the lad's not exactly the *sharpest* tool in the shed," and his daughter laughed until the tears rolled down her cheeks.

Nancy walked the rest of the way to the garbage container.

CHAPTER IV: AT A CROSSROAD

But upon arriving at the garbage container, instead of removing the lid, Nancy stood there, afraid of not finding the slipper after being so sure about the dragon-stain clue. It would mean that she was losing her touch. It would mean she had disappointed her father.

On the other hand, she was even more afraid of *finding* the slipper in there, for that would surely mean she was losing more than just her touch.

For a moment she considered not opening the lid at all. Her prunes were getting cold. Why not forget the whole business and go watch television?

But Nancy Drew was never one to give in to fear.

Taking her flashlight from the large pocket of her housecoat, she switched it on, then slowly lifted the lid. And there it was: her *hairbrush*.

"Oh, Father," she cried to the ceiling, "I miss you so!"

JAMEY'S SISTER

My dad hit me last night, twice, one side of the head and then the other—not very hard, but it was awful. He never hit me before, ever. For one thing I'm a girl, plus I'm already fifteen, so it's too late. Anyway, after those two little clouts he went over and took it out on the wall, making these horrible choking sounds.

I added it to the letter I'm always writing in my head to the president:

Mr. President, I wish you could have seen my dad last night. I wish you could see what he is going through, what we are all going through because of you.

Me and Jamey wrote to each other a lot before he died, not e-mails but regular letters in envelopes with stamps and all that. It was so exciting when one would come. Sometimes he put all our names on the envelope, in his bad handwriting: Mr. and Mrs. Carmichael and Melanie. But a lot of times it was just *my* name. He wrote about how hot it was over there, especially with all the stuff they had to wear and carry around, and about the guys he was with, his buddies he called them, and some of the things they would do to pass the time, goofy games they made up, because it got pretty boring a lot. He never talked about battles and such. He didn't want to worry us. All he would sometimes say was "Today was pretty bad," but he never went into details. He asked me a lot of questions to answer in my next letter, about school and such, basketball and such, and how he hoped I was having a lot of fun, that I should try to have enough fun for us both because *he* wasn't having much. Now and then, though, he'd say something about the way he felt being over there, how proud he was, serving his country, protecting it from another 9/11.

But Mr. President, Iraq wasn't the one. Saddam Hussein wasn't the guy. So why do you keep pretending like he was? What are you up to?

This girl at school, Miriam Holbrook, keeps telling me stuff. She's on the basketball team, our center. She's a senior and I'm just a sophomore but we ended up talking a lot after practice. She takes the same bus home and we got to talking about Iraq, especially after Jamey got killed. She's been telling me stuff you don't get from the news, the news on TV anyway. At first I didn't want to hear. She gets everything from her parents and they're both college professors. Those people are always against the government, always thinking they're smarter than everyone else.

Liberals.

My dad hates liberals. He thinks they should all be put in camps until the war is over so they won't be out there saying stuff that gives the enemy encouragement and gives our troops *dis*couragement. After the war is over they can come out again and shoot off their mouths all they want, but not until. Which is how I felt at first about Miriam and her parents. Lock them up. Shut them up.

But let's face it, Mr. President, you're the one who should be locked up. You're the one. You know you are.

At first, like I said, I told Miriam I didn't want to hear. I didn't call her a liberal or anything, I just told her I didn't want to hear it. She said she understood how I felt.

I told her no she didn't.

Jamey was the sweetest, most wonderful person I ever knew and I'm not just saying that because he was my brother but because it's totally true. Anyone who knew him would tell you the exact same thing. But Miriam never even met him. So when she said she understood, I looked at her and told her, "No, you don't."

She nodded. "You're right."

Well, I liked Miriam. She was a liberal but she shut up when you asked her to. So for a while we went back to just talking about school and basketball and Coach Murray's mood swings.

But I started noticing the president's eyes.

My dad has him on TV whenever he's on. Dad likes him a lot. He says we're lucky he was president when we got hit on 9/11. He says somebody like Bill Clinton, some liberal like Clinton, or Al Gore if he had won, they'd go running straight to the United

Nations and there'd be a lot of meetings and then they would have meetings about the meetings they had. But this president said, "Let's go get 'em." Dad had a picture of him on the living room wall above this little shrine he built to Jamey. He had this table against the wall with Jamey's picture in his marine dress blues, all his medals and documents laid out, even his varsity letter for baseball, little American flags all around. And up on the wall, smiling, a framed photograph of the president.

He has these eyes, did you ever notice?

He has these shifty little eyes. Know what he looks like? When he's up there in front of people, or talking into the camera, do you know what he looks like? A little boy, a naughty little boy telling lies, with a little trace of a smirk because he's getting away with it.

I told Miriam about his eyes. She just nodded. She knew what I meant. But then she changed the subject. We had a major game coming up and she talked about that. But I didn't care about the game coming up or Coach Murray or school or anything except the president and his shifty little beady eyes.

Or how cheerful he was.

I was watching him on my little TV in my room one night. He was answering questions from a roomful of reporters and I just kept praying, I actually had my hands pressed together, praying so hard for one of them to stand up and ask him how it feels when he thinks about all the people who are dead because of the lies he told. But they just asked about this and that, and he looked so cheerful up there, and used a nickname for someone he called on, calling him "Stretch," and everyone laughed, and he laughed too, kind of bobbing around with this smirky little chuckle, and I started screaming and couldn't stop. My mom came in and turned it off, then grabbed me and held me and I held her and we ended up crying together, just rocking and crying really hard.

But Mr. President, I don't want to cry. That's what everyone does, they just cry, all heartbroken but proud, so proud because their son gave his life to save his country. But as you know, Mr. President, that is bullshit, excuse my language but that is total fucking bullshit.

I told Miriam about being tired all the time.

We were on the bus. I was really bad at practice that afternoon, really sloppy. I couldn't focus. I felt so worn out. I told Miriam how hating the president was wearing me down. She didn't say anything. She just took my hand. No girl ever did that before, and a month ago I would have snatched it back, thinking she was a lesbian or something. But I let her hold it. We held hands all the way to my stop without talking.

They were watching a movie, Mom on the couch, Dad in his chair. I said hi and went to my room and laid on my bed on my back in the dark.

Jamey got blown up by a land mine. He stepped on a land mine and it blew his legs off. They helicoptered him to the hospital but he died on the way. That was what it said, "died en route." The last letter I got from him he talked about how soon he was going to be home, only six more weeks.

Mr. President, I don't know if Jamey knew about you and your lies. I hope not. I hope he still thought he was over there trying to keep us safe. I hope he died thinking he was protecting me, instead of how he got tricked by you, how we all did.

I fell asleep. I had this dream that Jamey was back. He was dead but he was allowed back, just for a visit. Then he would have to leave again, go back to being dead again. I kept asking him why he had to go back. I kept pestering him about it. I was totally ruining his visit. Then I woke up.

I was still in my clothes. It was late, after eleven. They were in bed. I got up to go pee. I was on my way to the bathroom, passing the Jamey shrine. It was lit up so you could see it no matter what time, Jamey in his uniform looking so proud, looking like a sucker, the president grinning from the wall above.

I took down the president and flung him across the room like a Frisbee. Then I swept my arm across the table, sending Jamey and his medals to the floor. Then I pulled the table down. Then Dad was there. He grabbed me and dragged me into my room and hit me with his open hand on one side of the head, then the other. Then he went over to the wall and started punching it and punching it, making these sobbing, choking sounds.

My mom came in and we went over to him. He had his forehead and his hands against the wall now, just crying, loud and horrible. We stood on either side of him, patting his shoulders and saying things.

Mr. President, do you know what you are? You are a monster. You don't have horns or hoofs or fangs or fur, but that is what you are, a monster.

That's how I try to think of him now. I try to think of him as some kind of monster instead of an actual human being. It's better that way. Otherwise I can't stand it. Otherwise I hate him so much I don't think I can stand it.

ABDUCTION

I was sitting there on the couch, a Saturday afternoon, feet up on the coffee table, watching the Cubs
lose another one. It was only the third inning and
already they were trailing the Braves 8–1. Do you
realize the Cubs haven't won a pennant since 1945?
Do you realize the Cubs haven't won a World Series
since 1908? This is 1980. That's seventy-two years.
And I'll tell you what, they're sure as hell not going
to win anything *this* year, not the way everyone keeps
swinging for the goddamn fence instead of just trying
to get on base, instead of trying to *manufacture* runs.
I don't know why I bother watching these losers, I
really don't. But anyway, like I was saying, the game
was in the third inning, bottom half, Cubs batting,
two outs, nobody on, then all of a sudden a bunch
of skinny little men with big bald heads and gigantic
eyes come marching and mumbling up to the couch
and start tickling me, digging their long bony fingers

in my ribs until I'm wiggling and giggling so hard I black out. Next thing I know, I'm waking up and it's the ninth inning, Cubs down 10–3.

I called up Jane.

"What do you want?" she says.

That's how she speaks to me these days. I deserve it. I fucked up. That's why I'm here in this little apartment. There was this lady barber, named Laura. I don't go there anymore, not since four haircuts ago. I go to this guy Lou or his partner Ted, whoever's there, it doesn't matter—they don't press their tits against my arm and whisper in my ear what a beautiful head of hair I've got, or finally one day go to the door and flip the OPEN sign to CLOSED and come walking back with a little smile on their face. By the way, I'm forty-one years old and although I still have all my hair I wouldn't necessarily call it beautiful, I'd call it gray. But who am I to argue with a barber?

Anyway, on the phone with Jane I tell her I'm not a hundred percent sure but I think I may have been abducted by aliens.

"What happened."

I tell her.

"They were *tickling* you?"

"Next thing I know, it's six innings later."

"And that's all you remember?"

"That's it."

"Sure you didn't just fall asleep and dream it?"

"It's possible."

"I would say *probable*."

"Right, you're the only one who gets abducted, the only one they ever choose."

"Jesus, Ed, listen to yourself, you sound just like a child."

Jane went to a hypnotist after she kept having these little "gaps." She's always been pretty spacey, but I told her if she was really worried she ought to go see a doctor. She had this theory, though, and went to a hypnotist who put her under and, sure enough, pulled out all these details about her being snatched away on a regular basis by aliens. She's never shared them with me, these details, but she's dropped a few hints. Apparently she has herself quite a good time up there. I asked her, was she talking about sex? She told me that's none of my business, not anymore. This has all happened, you see, in the last year or so, since we've been separated. The only definite thing she's told me concerning her abductors is that they're all marvelous dancers. So is Jane, as it happens. Or anyway, she thinks she is. We've gone dancing quite a lot over the years. I've never said anything but it's a little embarrassing how show-offy she gets on the floor, especially after a couple drinks.

She tells me now to try and describe what my visitors looked like.

"Very small, very skinny, with great big heads," I tell her.

"Bald?"

"Completely."

"And huge black eyes?"

"There you go."

"Hate to say it, Ed, but they sound like aliens out of a dozen different sci-fi movies."

"Yeah, well, *yours* sound like they're straight out of some beach party movie with Annette Funicello."

She laughed. Which is something I've always liked about Jane: she's not above laughing at herself sometimes.

"And what's-his-name, Tab Hunter," I added.

"Frankie Avalon," she corrected, and told me if I really wanted her to, she would come over and try hypnotizing me, find out what happened, if anything—"which I doubt very much," she added.

"Since when do you know how to hypnotize people?"

"I'll just do what *he* does. It doesn't involve much. You just have to trust whoever's doing it. Remember that word, Ed? 'Trust'?"

After we got off the phone I ran around the apartment picking up stuff, then jumped in the shower and afterwards got into all clean clothes, including underwear.

She knocked, just once.

When I opened the door she walked right past me, wearing this yellow sundress I like a lot. I told her how nice she looked.

"Yeah, yeah."

She had me sit on the couch while she sat on the coffee table facing me, our knees not quite touching. She held up a finger and moved it slowly left and right, telling me to keep my eyes on it. She said I was beginning to get very sleepy, that my eyelids were getting very heavy, that they were slowly closing, and I closed them slowly. She said I was falling into a sleep, into a deep sleep, into a very . . . deep . . . sleep. She asked me if I was asleep.

I answered in a sleepy voice, "Yes. I am."

But I wasn't.

I didn't want to go under. I was afraid to. On the phone she mentioned trust, right? Well, the truth was, I didn't trust her. She's still got quite a lot of anger over what happened, and I wasn't sure what she might do if given the chance, once she had me in her power. She might try to have some nasty fun with me, make me think I'm a monkey or a dog or a cat or something, have me *do* things, humiliating things.

But, see, I didn't want her to know I didn't trust her. So that's why I told her I was under, asleep.

"All right," she said, sounding kind of excited that it actually worked. "Now: I want you to tell me again. What happened? You were watching the ballgame, and then . . . ?"

"It was the third inning," I said in this slow, hypnotized voice, eyes closed. "The Cubs were losing, eight to one. They'd already made two pitching changes."

"Then what?"

"They were now batting. But instead of trying to get some runners on base, they were all swinging for the fence, they were all trying to—"

"Enough about the Cubs. You're sitting there watching the game. Then all of a sudden . . . ?"

"All of a sudden they came marching in, shoulder to shoulder, up to the couch, and started tickling me."

"And what do you remember next, Ed? What happened after that?"

She meant did I find myself on a flying saucer. Well, by now I was pretty certain I wasn't really abducted. The little men were just a goofy dream. I fell asleep, that's all. The Cubs will do that to you.

"Think, Ed."

Jane seemed to *want* me to remember being abducted. And I wanted it, too. It would be something exciting we could share, Jane with *her* aliens, me with mine—although, to be honest, I don't think Jane's been abducted any more than I have. But I know she likes to believe it. So this would be something to help us maybe reconnect a little. So I went ahead and made something up. I probably should have thought a little harder and come up with something better, but she was waiting, so I continued with the baseball theme and told her the next thing I knew I was sitting in a dugout.

"A *baseball* dugout, you're saying."

"Yes," I said. "That is correct."

"So . . . you were dreaming."

I told her no, that is *not* correct. I told her I was sitting there wearing a baseball uniform much too small for me and a cap that was much too large, and as I looked along the bench I saw all these little skinny guys with big heads, these aliens, my teammates.

"So you're saying you found yourself . . . on an alien baseball team."

"That is correct." Then I told her how *good* these guys played the game, how they played the old-fashioned way: drawing walks, bunting, hitting behind runners, stealing bases, *manufacturing* runs.

"Ed . . ."

I was into it now. It was the bottom of the ninth, I told her, two outs, we're down by a run, a guy on base, and they send me in to pinch hit. I go up there with this Little League–sized bat and take a nice easy swing, just trying to make contact, and what would have been a single in a human field turns out to be a home run, the field is so dinky. Game over, we win, and they're all waiting for me at home plate, jumping all over me, getting me down on the ground, tickling me, digging their fingers in, and the next thing I know . . . I'm back on the couch.

I kept my eyes closed, waiting.

She finally spoke. "That was a dream, Ed. You fell asleep during the game and had a very silly, juvenile, wish-fulfilling dream."

I tell her, "No. That is not correct."

"That *is* correct. You've wasted my time." She was quiet then. "Are you still under?" she asked.

"Yes," I said.

"Are you still seeing that woman, that . . . barber bitch?"

"No," I told her. "I am not."

Then she said, "I want you to tell me something, Ed."

"I will try."

"I want you to tell me exactly what it was about this woman that appealed to you. Will you tell me that please?"

"She liked my hair," I answered.

She was quiet for a second. "She liked your hair?"

"That is correct."

And it *is* correct. Right away, my very first time in the chair, Laura whispered in my ear, pressing a breast against my arm, "You have a beautiful head of hair, do you know that? So thick and luxurious," running her hand through it. She was quite a bit younger than me but seemed very excited by my hair—*sexually,* I'm saying. I felt like an exciting person, sexually and otherwise, like my hair was just the tip of the iceberg. I never cheated on Jane before, not even close. The whole time with Laura, I felt like I was out of my mind. That was the excuse I kept giving myself: *I'm out of my mind.* I started going for a trim every other Saturday, same time. Laura had this little room in the back of the shop, with a couch. I would usually sit and she would straddle me, her hands in my hair. We went on like that for six whole months. Then it was my birthday and Jane got me this incredible gift, a baseball signed by my guy, Ron Santo, former Cubs third baseman, a ballplayer with a tremendous heart. I couldn't stand it. I burst into tears and told her about Laura.

I still had my eyes closed as Jane said to me now, very calmly, very *factually*, "You are a piece of shit, Ed. You know that, don't you?"

"Yes," I said to her. "That is correct."

"A complete and utter piece of shit."

"That is correct."

"Stop saying that."

"All right."

She gave a sigh and said wearily, "Okay, I'm going to count to three and you'll wake up. One . . . two . . ."

I waited.

She was thinking, I could tell. Then she said, "I'm going to count to three and you will wake up wanting me so bad it hurts. You will be utterly, totally, pathetically desperate for me. You will be like a . . . like a pathetic little *dog.*"

See? What did I tell you? She wanted me to sit up and beg.

"Do you understand?" she said.

"I understand," I said.

"All right. One . . . two . . . three."

I opened my eyes, looked at her in that yellow sundress and began panting rapidly, my tongue hanging out. She stood up and moved away. I got down on all fours, intending to hump her leg.

"One-two-three you're *not* a dog, one-two-three you're *not* a dog," Jane kept telling me, backing off. But I *was* a dog, a miserable little mutt, and went on crawling towards her. And here's something sick: I had a terrific boner.

She backed up all the way to the door, groped for the knob, and found it. I stopped a few feet away. She was going to leave me now. She was going to go away and leave me here. I cocked my head and made whimpering sounds, begging to be taken home.

She let go of the doorknob.

I cocked my head to the other side, whimpering louder, meaning *Please? I'll be good. I'll be faithful and affectionate. I promise.*

"Oh, Eddie." She came over.

I wagged my butt.

She got down on the floor and stroked my hair, my luxurious gray fur.

DRACULA'S DAUGHTER

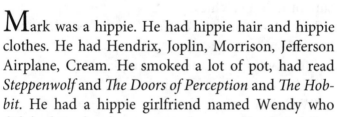

Mark was a hippie. He had hippie hair and hippie clothes. He had Hendrix, Joplin, Morrison, Jefferson Airplane, Cream. He smoked a lot of pot, had read *Steppenwolf* and *The Doors of Perception* and *The Hobbit*. He had a hippie girlfriend named Wendy who didn't shave her legs or even her armpits, hair being natural. So was sex. "Let's have sex, Mark," she would say, and he would say, "Let's," and they would. That was how natural.

Wendy lived in Stevenson North and Mark in South. He had a roommate named Steve, who was a nice guy but very straight, who talked about possibly pledging next semester. Wendy had a roommate named Maggie, who Mark still hadn't met. Wendy said she was kind of strange, but wouldn't say more than that.

There was a peace rally one Sunday afternoon at the lagoon. It was late October, a nice day out, windy but warm, the leaves on the trees flickering red and yellow. Mark and Wendy were going to the rally, of course—being for peace, being hippies.

He came to Wendy's room in his Buffalo Bill jacket, half the fringes missing, which he liked about it: showed he didn't care about appearances. Same with his Indian headband, half the beads gone. He was also wearing moccasins, but not to go with the headband, although of course Indians *were* the original hippies. On the left sleeve of the jacket he had a black armband, and when people asked him what it was for he told them, "For all the Vietnamese children we've burned and murdered."

Wendy was wearing her big, floppy straw hat. She looked cute in it, like a cute little hippie chick, *his* cute little hippie chick.

"Do I look all right in this?" she asked him. "Not too stylish?"

"You look like a cute little hippie chick."

"I don't want to look cute, Mark."

"Well, I'm sorry."

She told him to wait, she had to go pee. The bathroom was down the hall. Then they would leave. So he was waiting, studying the Salvador Dalí poster she had on the wall, the one with the melting clocks. Mark had never dropped acid. He was a little afraid it might be like this.

Then Maggie walked in.

He almost laughed.

He thought maybe she was on her way to a Halloween party, or back from one. It was nearly Halloween and he thought maybe this was her costume: Dracula's daughter, in a long black dress all the way to the floor, just a few inches longer than her shiny black hair. But her hair was real, you could tell, and her skin was so pale and her lips so full and shiny red and her arms so long and slender, and her eyebrows very low.

"Hello, Mark," she said, in a voice that came from deep in her throat, her long, white throat.

He had to swallow first before he could speak. "Hi," he said.

He wanted to sit down, his legs felt so weak, but then Wendy came back. She told Maggie they were on their way to the rally and asked if *she* had any plans for the afternoon.

Maggie said, "No." Then she looked at Mark, from under those eyebrows. "I'll be right here," she said, "all afternoon."

"Does she always dress like that?" he asked Wendy, on their way.

"Uh-huh."

When they got there, several hundred people were all sitting in the grass facing a platform set up in front of the west end of the lagoon, with a speaker system. Mark's political science teacher, Dr. Abernathy, was up there in a folding chair with several others, waiting to speak. At the microphone now was a student with a bleached-out denim jacket and acoustic guitar doing a song he wrote about the war, about the carnage, about Johnson's lies, about the military-industrial complex, a very long song that he sang in a Bob Dylan voice.

Sitting there next to Wendy, their legs folded under them, Mark was trying to pay attention to the song.

But he kept picturing that look Maggie gave him beneath her eyebrows, that deep, sly, knowing look: *I'll be here, Mark.* That was what she meant. *I'll be waiting for you.*

He didn't care about the carnage or Johnson's lies or the military industrial complex, or even about Wendy. *I'll be here, Mark.*

He got up, telling Wendy he had a cramp from sitting like that and wanted to walk it off, and went limping away before she could join him. He made his way in and out among all those solemn, earnest people sitting in the grass, whiffs of pot here and there, returning a lot of peace signs before he finally reached the sidewalk and took off running.

––––––––––

He knocked, softly.

"Come in, Mark."

He went in.

––––––––––

Afterward he wandered around the campus in a trance.

He ended up back at the rally, standing on the outskirts under a tree. Dr. Abernathy was at the microphone now, gesturing a lot, shouting against the strong wind. Wendy was sitting where he'd left her. She would lean forward and listen to Dr. Abernathy for a minute, then lean back and look around—for him, no doubt—then return to Dr. Abernathy.

In her hippie hat.

He wandered off toward the other side of the lagoon, no one over there. He could still hear Dr. Abernathy, going on now about napalmed Vietnamese children, the ones Mark was wearing his black armband for.

He slid it down off the sleeve of his Buffalo Bill jacket and flipped it away, then decided to get rid of the jacket as well and dropped it in the grass as he walked along. Same with the tie-dyed T-shirt underneath it, pulling it off over his head, the beaded headband coming with it. Next he kicked off his moccasins, left foot, right foot, pulled off his socks, then went ahead and unbuckled, unzipped, and slid his denim bell-bottoms down, along with his underpants, and stepped out of them. Still not satisfied, he got a good grip on his hair with both hands and pulled his entire suit of skin off over his head—guts and muscles sliding from his bones into a warm heap.

This was more like it.

He walked on, the wind making eerie music in his ribs.

KILLING CARL

He was my girlfriend Cindy's husband, so what else could I do? I guess I could have *not* killed him. Anyway, it's too late. I got him with a .22 pistol, a pretty wimpy gun but I got him in the middle of the forehead three inches away. We were standing around in his office, everyone else gone home, talking about the White Sox, agreeing what they need is pitching, hitting, and fielding, and then they'd be set. "Oh, by the way," I said, and pulled out the gun and shot him. You should have seen the look on his face. Talk about surprised. But only for a second, then his eyes went blank. He was already dead when he hit the floor, otherwise he would have hurt himself the way he fell, broke his arm or something, which maybe he did, but that was minor compared to being dead.

I told him I was sorry. I told him I didn't really mean it. I was even crying a little. I never killed anyone before. It's not as enjoyable as you might think. I said to him, "Carl, can you forgive me?" He didn't answer. I took that as a yes and got out of there. I didn't want to be around when the authorities arrived, him lying there dead, me standing over him with the so-called smoking gun. That would look pretty suspicious. I drove to my apartment and walked around and around. I couldn't believe Carl was really gone—I was just talking to him twenty minutes ago! I was in denial, you see. But then I accepted it. That's the first step, acceptance. Then I had to learn to forgive myself. "I forgive you," I said, and I meant it. I figured if *Carl* could forgive me, right?

I called up Cindy. "He's dead."

"Butter wouldn't melt in *your* mouth."

"What does that mean?"

"I don't know. This is so upsetting."

"I thought you'd be pleased."

"He had some good points, Sid."

"Name one."

"He had a nice smile."

"A *lot* of people have a nice smile. *I* have a nice smile, for crying out loud."

"You think?"

"I've been told."

"Not by me."

"You don't think I have a nice smile?"

"I'm trying to picture it. Are you smiling now?"

"Cindy, I just killed a man, a fellow human being!"

"Well, how do you think *I* feel? He was my husband!"

"You're right. I'm sorry."

"Did he say anything?"

"He forgave me."

"Good old Carl."

"Don't start."

"Sorry."

"I just hope they don't find out who did it, that's all."

"*He's* not gonna tell."

We laughed pretty hard at that one.

"You're a nut," I told her, "you know that?"

"Why don't you come over and crack me open?"

I did.

Afterwards we sat up and watched a courtroom drama. One of the lady lawyers made Cindy look like a bag of last week's dog shit. But what can you do? Love, explain love. Hell, explain anything.

Has the jury reached a verdict?

"Turn it off," Cindy told me.

We have, Your Honor.

"Turn it off!"

I turned it off.

"Sid, I'm scared. Hold me. *Hold* me."

I held her.

"Promise me we'll never part!"

I promised.

"Promise me you'll say it was all your fault, I had nothing to do with it!"

I promised. I told her I didn't care if they gave me the hot seat, let 'em.

She laughed. "'The hot seat.' They'll give you an injection, Sid. You won't even feel it."

"Yeah? *Here's* an injection," I said, and pounced on her. "Can you feel *this*?"

"Oh, Sid, oh yes, oh God, oh yes, oh darling yes, oh fuck me hard, oh Sid, oh yes!"

Afterwards I accused her of faking it.

She accused me of murder.

We decided to get out of town. We couldn't agree on the direction, though. We were in Homewood, Illinois, and she wanted to head to Southern California: movie stars roller-skating under palm trees. I wanted to go to Maine: rocks and lobsters. I was driving, so we headed east. "When it's your turn to drive we can head for California, that's up to you," I said. "But right now I don't want to hear any more about Johnny fucking Depp. Is that understood?"

Cindy loves it when I get bossy. She started working on my zipper. So now I'm driving along the highway on a lovely summer evening getting slurpy road-head, thinking *This is living! This is what the TV commercials are all about!* And now I'm not even thinking because the top of my head is coming off.

Then I hear the siren.

"Aw shit, Cindy, get off! Come on! We gotta make a run for it!"

"No, Sid! Don't!"

"We're wanted for murder!"

"We're wanted for speeding!"

She was right. I pulled over.

"Sid."

"What."

"Your dick is out."

"Christ."

The officer came up and bent over so his big freckled face was at the window saying something I couldn't hear, so I rolled down the window, which was probably what he was saying.

He asked me if I knew how fast I was going.

I told him, "A whole lot faster than I *should* have been, sir, I know that. And I just want to say how sorry I am. I mean that sincerely."

"That goes for both of us, Officer," Cindy told him, leaning over me. "We're ashamed of ourselves." She started crying into my lap really hard.

"There, there," I said, patting her head. "He understands, honey. He understands."

"Can I see your license, please?"

I said, "Sure thing, Officer." Cindy got off my lap. "Let me just . . ." I had the gun in my coat pocket, but then I thought *Nah* and gave him my license.

He went back to the car with it.

Cindy whispered, "Jeez, it's not like you *killed* somebody."

We started giggling.

"*Shh!*"

"*Shh!*"

We couldn't stop. By the time he came back we were helpless, like a couple of drunks. So now he told me to step out of the car please.

Which wasn't quite so funny.

I told him, "*Sorry, gotta run,*" and took off, spitting gravel in his face, Cindy giving a whoop and a holler.

"This is it!" I shouted. "This is it!"

I'm doing seventy . . . I'm doing eighty . . .

"Fuck me, Sid! Fuck me!"

"Not right now, honey!"

I'm up to ninety, ninety-five, nudging a hundred, laying on the horn, letting Jesus know we're coming, letting Him know we're on our way!

The Creature from the Black Lagoon

Eve honey, dear fiancée of mine,

I'm going to call you as soon as I'm allowed, but meanwhile I want to say some things I can't say over the phone. First of all, honey, do you know how I feel right now? Like the Creature from the Black Lagoon. Remember that movie? Sitting on the couch together, sharing a bowl of popcorn, thinking this will be good for some laughs? Remember, though? How sad it was?

Anyway, please apologize to your family for me. Explain how drunk I was. And mention what I just said, about feeling like a monster.

I can hear your mother: "Well, he is a monster."

Tell her I agree, completely.

You might add, however, that an actual monster probably wouldn't be calling himself a monster. So I guess maybe I'm not a complete monster, although to be honest I almost wish I was—no shame, no remorse. Might be kind of nice.

I want to explain the way it happened, Eve.

Swimming around like that in your parents' pool, back and forth underwater, while you and your mom and dad and Adam were all sitting at the patio table looking through photos from the happy days before I came along, I began feeling like—you guessed it—the Creature from the Black Lagoon. Remember how he looked in the water? So beautiful and wild and free. But alone. So alone. Okay, so then I happened to come up for air and you're all laughing hysterically over some picture, and I just wanted to be a part of it, in the picture so to speak, that's the only reason I took off my trunks and swung them over my head shouting "Woo-hoo" like that, just to be part of the general hilarity. The water was up to my waist, so I wasn't actually exposing myself and I honestly thought you would all just laugh and shake your heads at what a lovable nut I was. Instead, the four of you sat there with the exact same look on all your faces—outrage, anger, and disgust—your father ordering me out of the pool and off his property like I was some kind of intruder, which, let's face it, I was. And please believe me, sweetheart, I had every intention of putting my trunks back on before getting out, but the way your brother followed up your father with "Right now, mister," I decided fine, have it your way.

I hope your mother has recovered, I mean that sincerely. But I have to say, it did seem a little theatrical, her crying out "Oh dear God in heaven" and fainting? Actually <u>fainting</u>?

Also, just for the record, when your brother got up and came after me, the only reason I hurried to the car like I did was because, as you well know, I do not believe in violence as a way to resolve differences. Good thing, too. Desperate naked creature from the water that I was, I'm pretty sure I would have seriously injured him.

Anyway, if it helps at all, let me once again repeat how sorry I am, how truly, deeply, profoundly fucking sorry. I just hope you're able to see things a little bit from my perspective, that's all, from down here in the Black Lagoon.

Long story short, driving home I got pulled over for speeding, tried to get into my trunks in time, didn't make it. So now I'm wearing orange pajamas.

Eve, do you remember the end of the movie? After they shoot the creature and he goes staggering back to the water, swims a little distance, then sinks to the murky bottom—do you remember what you said?

"All he wanted was to be loved."

Do you remember saying that, Eve?

—Gordon

FRANKENSTEIN
AND HIS MOM

———··◁∞▷··———

Dumpy Mrs. Wilcox and her scrawny eighteen-year-old, Paul, watched the 1931 *Frankenstein* in the den one night. At the end of the movie, when the peasants set fire to the windmill with the monster trapped inside, Mrs. Wilcox said, "Good riddance to bad rubbish."

But Paul felt like weeping.

Later in his room before going to bed he searched in his closet and found the rubber Frankenstein mask he'd worn for Halloween several years ago and put it on in front of the dresser mirror.

How pitiful he looked, how sad and tragic. He held out his arms as if to say, *I didn't ask for this. I didn't ask for any of this.*

———

"Yoo-hoo," his mother called from the kitchen the next morning. "Pauley, breakfast, let's go, come on, get out here, *now*."

He walked in wearing pajama bottoms, T-shirt, and Frankenstein mask.

Mrs. Wilcox gave a cry, dropped the box of Alpha-Bits she was bringing to the table, and stepped backward against the countertop, holding her heart.

Paul sat down.

His mother picked up the box of cereal—none of the letters had spilled out—and set it on the table. "Are you trying to kill me, hon? Give me a seizure?" She sat across from him. "Or simply drive me out of my mind, send me right around the bend—is that your intention? Because if it is, I can tell you right now, you're doing a marvelous job."

He poured milk over his Alpha-Bits, then inserted a spoonful of letters through the mouth-opening in the mask.

Reaching for the box she told him, "You've got milk on the chin."

He used his napkin.

––––––––

Later he was at his desk with a pen and notebook number seventeen of his journal, "Reflections in a Broken Mirror":

> *Been wearing a Frankenstein mask since I got up, not sure why. Watched the movie last night. Boris Karloff. So sad! At the end Mom says, "Good riddance." I had the mask on when I came into the kitchen for breakfast, scared the shit out of her. She couldn't see me smiling.*

Mrs. Wilcox knocked on the locked door. "Paul, I'm going to the store. Did you want anything?"

"Corn chips, big bag."

"I might be a while. I'll probably stop at Saint Pat's to light some candles to Our Lady."

"All right."

"Three of them. Would you like to know what for?"

"That's okay."

"One for myself, for peace of mind. Then one for your father, for his soul. And then a candle for my son, that someday he gets himself a job. That's my number-three candle. Number one, peace of mind. Number two, your father's soul. Number three, Paul gets a job."

"I've been looking."

"No, dear, you haven't. You haven't been looking at all. You went to that interview a week ago Wednesday for that night watchman's job and that's been it."

"I'm waiting to hear from the guy."

"Meanwhile you could be out looking somewhere else."

"I want to be here when he calls."

"Didn't you give him your cell phone number?"

"I forgot to."

She was quiet out there for a moment. Then: "Paul, I'm beginning to think you don't really *want* to find a job."

"No, I do. I'm very hopeful. Got my fingers crossed," he told her, crossing his fingers.

"Then how about this? Call the man today and tell him—or better yet, go *in* there today and say to him, 'Look, sir, am I going to get this job or not? Because

if I'm not, I need to be looking elsewhere.' Put it to
him like that. He might admire that kind of attitude."

"That's a good idea. I should probably wait until
next week, though. Don't wanna start pestering the
guy too soon, jeopardize my chances."

"Oh, Paul . . ."

"*What.*"

"You're so full of it."

"Right. Fine. I'll go in there today. I'll get dressed
and go in and piss the guy off—"

"You haven't dressed yet?"

"—and lose whatever chance I've got—"

"Are you still in your pajamas?"

"—so you can keep me here under your wing—
under your *thumb*, I should say."

"Oh, stop it. Nothing in this world would please me
more than to see you in your own apartment feeding
yourself and you know that."

"The guy said there was a definite opening."

"The *newspaper* said that much."

"*And*—if you'll let me finish?"

"Listening."

"He said he liked my attitude."

"Oh?"

"He said I seemed like a real . . . you know . . ."

"A real what, hon."

"A real go-getter."

Mrs. Wilcox burst out laughing. It took her a while
to stop. "I'm sorry," she managed to say.

"Glad I amuse you."

"That you do, hon."

"Corn chips, big bag."

"Paul?"

"What."

"Are you still wearing that Halloween mask? Your voice sounds like you still have it on."

He didn't answer.

"Are you in there wearing that silly mask, hon?"

He still didn't answer.

"Paul?"

"*Go to the fuckin' store, Ma, will ya?*"

Silence.

"Sorry," he said.

Silence.

"Bad word," he admitted.

She finally spoke, quietly and carefully: "I know you're probably not very happy, Paul. I know that." She paused. "But, hon? Don't ever use that word in my house again. *Ever.* Do you understand? Or else, do you know what, Paul? I won't let you live here anymore. You'll have to live somewhere in a cardboard box. You'll have to be a big, potty-mouthed monster out on the sidewalk in a box: no electricity, no running water, no TV, no corn chips. I don't think you would like your new home."

"I said I'm sorry."

"I know you did and I know you are, but that word, Paul. Not in my house. Not from my only child . . . whom I nursed at my breast . . ."

"Don't," he said quietly.

"Oh, hon . . ."

"Please?" he whispered.

"Remember how I used to sing to you? Do you remember? *Ohhh, the itsy bitsy spider went up the water spout . . .*"

Paul got to his feet and stood there making angry Frankenstein sounds toward the door, stiffly swinging his arms around. Then he sat down again.

She was quiet. Then she asked him, "Was that supposed to be Frankenstein, hon? Is that what you're doing now, turning into Frankenstein?"

"Corn chips, Mom," he said, weakly. "Will you?"

"I'm going, I'm going."

"Big bag."

"Right," she said, walking off. "Big bag for the big monster."

He returned to his notebook:

Interesting little exchange with her just now . . .

––––––––

He had finished writing and was carefully drawing a lanky naked woman with heavy-lidded eyes when his mother knocked and sang out, "Got your corn chips, hon."

"Thank you."

"Do you want them now?"

"That's all right."

"Listen, Paul, I was thinking. What if we had a dog? A great big friendly dog. Would you like that? You could take him down to the park and throw things and he would bring them back in his mouth—what's the word for that?"

"'Fetch.'"

"He would fetch things, sticks and rubber balls and things. I was thinking you could call him Buster. Paul and his dog Buster. Would that . . . you know . . . help, do you think? If we had a dog?"

Paul turned in his chair and spoke toward the door: "I would kill it."

"No, you wouldn't, honey. Don't say that."

"I would kill it and eat it."

"You're not like that, Paul. You know you're not. This is just a phase you're going through. All young people go through phases. This is just your . . . well, your Frankenstein phase, that's all. You wouldn't kill an innocent dog, Paul." She paused. "Would you?"

He threw back his head and laughed.

"Oh, it's nice to hear you laugh, hon."

———

They sat across from each other eating lunch—La Choy chicken chow mein—Paul still in his pajamas, T-shirt, and Frankenstein mask, dumping salt all over his plate.

"Why don't you taste it, hon, before you . . ." She sighed.

They ate.

Paul stabbed a nickel-sized disc and held up his fork. "What're these?"

"That's a . . . what's it called . . . a *water* chestnut."

"Is it food?"

"Of course it's food, what do you think?"

He put it in the mouth slot of the mask, chewed, and shook his head. "Hundred percent taste-free."

"Well, dump another pound of salt on your plate."

He did that.

"Just thought I'd try making something a little different," she said. "You don't have to eat everything. I know how scary new food can be."

"I wasn't scared. All I said—"

"Fear of the unknown," she said in a spooky voice.

"I wasn't *scared*, okay?"

"Don't shout at me, Paul."

They ate.

"Your *father* was the most narrow-minded eater I ever saw. He thought anything on his plate besides meat was just . . . what's the word I want . . . not 'decoration' . . ."

"'Garnish.'"

"*Garnish*. Couldn't think of it."

She was quiet then.

He went on eating.

"That's been happening to me a lot lately, Paul," she said after a minute. "A blank spot where a word should be. Like 'garnish,' or . . . what was it earlier I couldn't think of, when you throw things for a dog . . ."

"'Fetch,'" he said with his mouth full.

"That was it. Now, I ask you, is that such a difficult word?"

He went on eating.

"Paul, what if I'm . . . oh God, hon, what if I'm coming down with . . . what's it called . . . when you lose your mind . . ."

"Alzheimer's."

"See? I couldn't think of it!" She laid down her fork and sat there with her hands in her lap, staring off.

Paul stabbed another water chestnut and held it up. "What're these called again?"

She looked. "Water chestnuts."

"Oh yeah." He put it in his mouth. "Couldn't think of it."

She nodded at him, smiling softly, as he went on eating. "You're a nice boy, Paul. Do you know that?"

"All right."

"Whether you like it or not, you're a very nice—"

"All *right*."

"Don't shout at me, hon."

"I wasn't shouting."

"Well, don't."

They ate.

———

"I wish he would grow back his mustache," Mrs. Wilcox said from her end of the couch. "I liked him so much better in a mustache."

Sprawled at his end, still in his pajamas and mask, a large bag of corn chips between his thighs, Paul said, "Peter Pan."

"Question, hon," she reminded him. "In the form of a question."

They watched.

"Amelia Earhart," he said.

"*Who*, Paul, *who* is Amelia Earhart."

"Aviator."

"No, I'm saying . . . never mind."

They watched.

"He's Canadian, you know," she told him, as she did every time. "They're very sophisticated, Canadian men."

They watched.

She laughed. "And I love his sense of humor. Very dry, very Canadian. Like their ginger ale."

They watched.

"Oh I *know* this one," she said. "Small, blonde, very cute, oh God what is her name?" She sagged. "Meg Ryan. Of course." She looked at Paul. "See, hon? How I'm getting?"

He placed a corn chip through the mouth of the mask.

"If I find one corn-chip crumb on this couch, so help me God," she promised.

A shampoo commercial came on, a beautiful red-haired woman staring deep into Paul's eyes as she told him she deserves it. He squirmed just a little.

"Pretty girl, isn't she?" his mother said, and looked at him. "Very attractive, don't you think?"

"Quit it."

When the show came back Mrs. Wilcox clicked her tongue. "I hate this, where he talks to them." She picked up the remote from her lap and studied it. "Where's the mute on this one? I can never . . . here it is." She pressed a button. "That's better." She began speaking for the contestant, a tall woman in narrow glasses. "Well, Alex," she said in a fussy voice. "Once? I was getting on a bus? And I didn't have the exact change? And the driver wouldn't let me on? And I said 'Oh no' and ran home and got some change and waited for the next bus? And by the time I got to work? I was almost late!"

Paul chuckled quietly. "What's *this* one saying?"

"Him? Well. *He's* telling Alex all about the time when he was a little boy and his mother caught him going through her dresser looking at her *underwear*, at her bras and her soft, pretty panties, feeling with his fingers, and she gave him such a spanking on his cute little bare behind he couldn't sit down for a week, not for a *week*, Alex."

Paul was slouching now almost horizontal.

"And *this* one," his mother went on, as Alex stepped over to the champion, "*he's* telling Alex all about the time he cheated on his young wife and she caught him and it turned out it wasn't the first time and he ended up joining the marines, even though she was three months pregnant, and got himself blown up in some godforsaken place called Beirut, and yet here he is, a three-time returning champion."

She aimed the remote and pressed a button for the sound.

Along with the tall woman in glasses Paul ran the entire column of classic movie quotes. There was applause from the audience, his mother joining in while sadly shaking her head: "Oh, hon, it breaks my heart, it really does. Someone so special, so gifted, yet here he sits, in his pajamas, in a *Halloween* mask, in the middle of the afternoon, watching a game show with his mommy. I tell ya, Paul, it just about breaks my—"

With a Frankenstein roar he got to his feet, the bag falling from his lap, corn chips spilling onto the carpet. He stepped on them as he lurched off, stiffly waving his arms all around.

"Oh, that's right, I forgot!" she hollered, getting up and following him, her face thrust forward. "You never *had* a mommy, you were assembled by a mad scientist, I keep forgetting!"

He closed the door in her face, locked it, and went lurching and waving his arms all around the room.

"And he put the wrong brain in your head," she went on, "from the wrong jar, the brain of a lazy loafer who lives off his mother while treating her like she's some kind of pest, some kind of nuisance! But that's not *your* fault, is it. It's not *your* brain, it's someone *else's*. How convenient, Paul, how very convenient!" she shouted, then returned to the den and the rest of *Jeopardy!*

Paul stood there. Then he sat at his desk and took up his pen:

> *I hate when she thinks she's <u>on</u> to me, like she has me all figured out. What does she think, I <u>enjoy</u> wearing this thing? It's hot and has a nauseating rubber smell, that's how much I enjoy it. She doesn't know me. Nobody does. I didn't ask for this, for <u>any</u> of this.*

The telephone out in the living room rang.

He waited, listening.

"Hello?" she said. Then: "May I ask who's calling?"

Oh Jesus.

"Just a moment please, I'll see if he's in."

Oh Jesus.

She came and knocked. "Paul, telephone," she said, low and urgent. "It's a Mr. Cooper, about the job. He wants to talk to you. I think he wants to take you, hon. Hire you. Should I tell him to hold on, you'll be right there? My son's been hoping to hear from you? Is that what you want me to say?"

He didn't answer.

"Paul? Honey?"

"What."

"Is that what you want me to tell him, that you really *want* this job? This is something you really want to do? Walk around all night in a gloomy warehouse? Aren't you gloomy *enough*, hon?"

He turned around in his chair and looked at the door.

"Should I tell him you're not home? You're down at the park with your dog, Buster, throwing a stick so he can bring it back in his mouth—what's the word again for that? So I can tell him."

"'Fetch,'" he said.

"'Fetch.' Couldn't think of it. That's been happening to me a lot lately, have I told you? I don't remember. See what I mean? And now I can't remember the man's name on the phone!"

"Cooper."

"That was it. I'll tell him, 'I'm sorry, Mr. Cooper, but Paul is down at the park playing fetch with his dog Buster. He loves that dog. And he loves his mother. He doesn't think he does but he does. And I love my son. He's a good boy, Mr. Cooper, a sweet boy, and I'm sorry but you can't have him. So thank you for calling, have a nice day.' That's what I'll say to him, Paul, that's what I'll tell him," she said, heading back to the phone.

Paul stood up and yanked off the mask, crying "*Waaait!*"

OSCAR

It was a pleasant early-September evening. I had the car window down, elbow out, a block and a half away from my condo, coming home from work. I'm an attorney at Hampton and Chandler, specializing in wills and estate taxes, been there less than three years and already I'm being mentioned for an associate partner. The car hit a bump. I was busy with the radio—this song I like was on but there was static, so I was fiddling with the dial and took my eyes off the road and hit this bump, which cleared the static—and I shouted out the chorus:

You! Shook me all! Night! Long!
Yeah you! Shook me all! Night! Long!

I pulled up in front of my condo but stayed in the car finishing the song:

You really took me and you!
Shook me all! Night! Long!

Afterwards I'm in the condo, humming the song, hanging up my tie, my suit jacket, trying to decide whether or not to take a quick shower before picking up Megan, just to get rid of the office. Megan was my fiancée, Megan Chandler, the boss's lovely daughter. We were getting married October 23rd, reception at Ramada Inn, Aruba for the honeymoon, then a house in Glenview, two kids, boy and a girl, Scott Jr. and Brittany, perhaps a Siamese cat named Cleo. For tonight, though, we had dinner reservations at Raoul's, afterwards a movie—we hadn't decided which one, something to discuss over dinner.

There was a loud knock at the door—more of a *kick*, actually.

I went over and looked through the peephole. It was Pinkie. That was how I thought of her, this very overweight woman who lives a couple blocks up the road in a trailer painted bright pink, who always dresses in pink, usually in what she was wearing now, this pink sweatsuit. Looking through the peephole it took me a couple moments to figure out what she was holding in her arms. It was this little wiener dog of hers. It was dead. There wasn't any gore that I could see, but it was dead all right, the way it was lying so limp. Pinkie was sobbing.

I opened the door. "Help you?"

"Monster!"

"Beg pardon?"

"Monster!"

"Please explain why you're calling me that."

She held out the dog. "You did this!"

"I killed your dog? What're you, nuts?"

"You ran over him and just kept going! Singing away!"

That bump in the road.

I apologized, sincerely. I told her I certainly hadn't *meant* to run over the thing, that I hadn't even known, and if I *had* known I certainly wouldn't have gone on singing. I also pointed out that if her dog was going to be running around in the street, she needed to realize the driver can in no way be held liable, provided he was going the speed limit, which I was.

She repeated I was a monster.

I took out my wallet. "Let me at least reimburse you. I'm not legally *bound* to, not in any way, but I would *like* to. Forty, would you say?"

She stared at me.

"Sixty?"

"Monster!"

I put my wallet back. "All right, look. I'm very sorry about your dog—did it have a name, by the way?"

"Oscar!"

"I'm very sorry about Oscar and I mean that sincerely, but as it happens I'm running a little late right now, so let me just say once again how truly sorry I am and that I hope you can find a way to move on from this unfortunate, purely accidental tragedy," gradually closing the door in her face.

"Monster!"

I looked through the peephole. After giving the door a final kick she went away, Oscar in her arms. I went over to the couch and flopped there on my back. "Jesus," I whispered, still seeing that fat, red face calling me a monster.

The phone on the glass coffee table rang.

I let the machine answer it, in case it was dead dog related. It was Megan. "Hi, sweetheart," she said. She'd been calling me that for about a month now, ever

since we got engaged. I thought I liked it but now it
made me cringe a little. "Just checking to make sure
we're still on for tonight," she said. "You'll be by at
six thirty, right?"

I picked it up. "Right. See you then."

"Guess what I'm going to wear."

"No idea. I'll see you then."

"Scott?"

"Yeah?"

"What's the matter?"

"Nothing."

"*Some*thing."

I told her, "I just had a very . . . bizarre encounter."

"Oh?"

"This woman down the road came by."

"A woman? What woman?"

"*A big fat woman in a pink sweatsuit, all right?*"

"Why are you shouting at me?"

"Sorry."

"A big fat woman . . ." she prompted.

"With a dead dog in her arms."

She was quiet for a moment. "A big fat woman
with a dead dog in her arms came by?"

"Apparently I killed the thing."

"No."

"Yes."

"How? What happened?"

"I ran over it."

"Oh God, with your car?"

"Yes, Megan, with my *car*."

"Scott, you're yelling at me again."

"I thought it was a bump in the road. I didn't think
it was a *dog*."

"Did you explain to her?"

"I tried to. She just kept calling me a monster."

"Well . . . I'm sure she didn't mean it. She was just upset."

"I even offered to pay for the thing."

"Pay for the dog?"

"I went up to sixty dollars."

"Scott . . ."

"What the hell *else* could I do?"

"Did you at least say you were sorry?"

"Of course I did."

"And were you?"

"What the hell *is* this, Megan?"

"I would like to know, Scott. Did you feel bad?"

"For the woman, you mean?"

"Did you?"

I thought about it. "I guess I would have to say . . . no, not especially."

She didn't say anything.

"Maybe if she didn't keep calling me a monster, you know?"

"What about the dog?"

"What about it?"

"Did you feel bad for the *dog* at least?"

"You're starting to piss me off, Megan, you know that?"

"Well, I'm sorry. It's just . . . I mean . . ."

"What. You mean what."

"You didn't care about the woman . . . didn't care about the dog . . ."

"And you're wondering if maybe she was right about me."

"I don't think you're a monster, Scott."

"Well, thank you. That's about the nicest thing anyone's ever said to me."

We were quiet. This was our first real argument.

"Can I ask you something?" she said.

"Go ahead."

"Do you love me?"

I thought about it.

"Scott?"

"Let me get back to you," I said, and hung up.

What a feeling!

I walked all around the apartment, arms spread
wide. "If I am a monster, then I shall *be* one!" I
declared, actually using the word "shall."

The phone rang.

I let it. Megan came on, crying now. "Scott, please
pick up? We need to talk. Sweetheart, please? Don't
do this? Please don't do this to us?"

She sounded so pathetic I hurried over, but she
hung up before I could get there.

I started poking her number, thinking, I'll tell her
how sorry I am, that I was upset, the dead dog, all that,
I'll be over at six thirty, we'll go to Raoul's, afterwards
a movie, get married next month, fly to Aruba. Before
punching the last number I looked off, pictured us
lying side by side on the beach: *This is so wonderful,
Scott, isn't it? Scott? Isn't it?*

I set the phone back down.

I sat on the couch.

I got up and walked around.

I sat on the couch again.

I got up and left the apartment.

I headed on down the road. It was a pleasant evening, as I mentioned. I knocked on Pinkie's trailer. I
wasn't sure what I wanted. I knocked again, louder.

"Back here!" she hollered.

I went around the back. There was a small yard,
hardly any grass, mostly just bare dirt and dog turds.
Pinkie was whacking down a smallish mound with the
back of a shovel. She looked up and I stopped walking.
She went back to work and I stepped up closer.

She tossed away the shovel. "Kneel," she told me.

"Beg pardon?"

She got down on her knees on the other side of
the little mound, put her hands together, and looked
at me, waiting.

I checked around my feet for dog turds, got down,
and folded my hands.

She lifted her eyes towards Heaven. "Lord? I don't
know whether dogs are allowed in Your Kingdom, I
don't know your pet policy, but I'm asking You to
let Oscar through those gates. He won't give You any
trouble, Lord, I guarantee. He was a good little dog, a
happy little fella. He got run over by this young man
right here. He says he didn't mean it, says he didn't
even know, too busy singing away, singing so loud
he couldn't hear the screams of a little dog he was
crushing to death, a sweet little creature who never
hurt anyone, Lord, who just wanted to run around
and play, that's all, just run around and play in the
sun. Oh look, Lord. He's crying."

She came over and helped me up. She walked me to
the trailer, into her little pink-tiled kitchen, sat me
down at a pink Formica table, and poured us both

some coffee. She asked me if I meant what I'd said earlier about sixty dollars. She'd like to buy a headstone.

I gladly got my wallet out and laid three twenties down.

We drank our coffee and considered what the headstone ought to say. She went and got a pen and paper. I suggested something simple: *Here lies Oscar, a good little dog.*

She wrote that down. "Or how about this?" she said, writing it: "*Here . . . lies . . . Oscar . . . a . . . good . . . little . . . dog . . . killed . . . by . . . a . . . monster.*"

"Perfect," I told her, getting up. "Says it all."

"Where you going?"

"For a walk, stretch my legs."

"Monster!"

Strolling along the side of the road, hands behind my back, kicking a stone ahead of me, I felt bad for Pinkie and hoped she got herself another little companion real soon. I also felt bad for Megan and hoped *she* got herself another companion soon. Meanwhile, the sun was sinking very colorfully, a soft little breeze coming up. And as I walked along I mostly felt bad for poor little Oscar, having to leave such a pleasant world as this.

The Weary Ghost
of Uncle Doug

———··◄∞►··———

I woke up in the middle of the night and there he
was, sitting on the edge of the bed in the moonlight
from the window, in his lumberjack shirt, staring off.
I was about to scream—but he looked so sad, sitting
there shaking his head.

"Uncle Doug?" I said.

He gave a long sigh.

I got up on my elbows. "What're you doing here?"

Another sigh.

"What's the matter? Tell me."

"A friend of mine," he said, still looking off, "I forget
his name . . . this was long ago . . . told me to buy
up all the shares I could in a young company . . . a
camera company . . . and do you know the name of
that camera company?"

"Kodak," I said.

"And I was going to. I had fifty dollars at the time
and I was going to buy fifty dollars' worth of shares

in Kodak, at eighteen cents a share. That's a lot of shares, Tommy." He looked at me. "But do you know what I did with that money? Instead?"

"Went to the track," I said.

He looked off again. "Someone else had given me a *different* tip, you see. I still remember the name of the horse: Gypsy Queen. I put fifty dollars to win on Gypsy Queen, and do you know where she finished? Where my Gypsy Queen came in?"

"Eighth," I said.

"In a field of nine," he added, and sat there shaking his head.

I sat up further. "Uncle Doug, you told me that story a hundred times while you were alive. You're not still going over that *now*, are you? You've been dead for ten years."

"Gypsy . . . Queen."

"Uncle Doug?"

"There's nothing else to do here."

"Where . . . exactly *are* you?"

He shook his head. "Not a clue."

"So you just wander around regretting you didn't buy shares in Kodak?"

He nodded.

"That's awful. Can't you just let go of it?"

"I don't want to," he said.

"You *want* to go around beating yourself up till the end of time?"

"You don't understand, Tommy. Otherwise I'll just drift away, just . . . *merge*. Jesus, I hate that word."

"Merge with the elements, you mean?"

"With the sky and the trees and the sheep and the sheep shit and the goddamn *flies* on the sheep shit— yeah, all that."

"But that's a *good* thing, Uncle Doug. That's . . . you know, organic."

He looked at me. "I don't ever want to forget myself."

"But . . . you're *miserable*."

He turned away. "Nevertheless." He sat there looking off, stubbornly.

I had an idea. "How about if I promise *I'll* never forget you, Uncle Doug—how would *that* be? Then you could let go and I'll still be here remembering."

He sighed. "I *am* awful tired, Tommy."

"I would think."

"So," he said, "what would you remember?"

"Well, let's see . . ."

"I ever tell you about that time I was in the service? What I did to that smart-assed corporal?"

"Knocked him ass over teakettle, as I recall."

"What about that smart-ass of a *foreman* I had?"

"Ass over teakettle. You've told me all your stories, Uncle Doug, and I promise I'll never forget them. They're easy to remember. So you might as well go ahead and . . . you know . . ."

"Join the sheep shit?"

"You might as well."

He sat there looking off. Then he suddenly thrust his sleeve at me. "Speaking of sheep, feel that material."

I felt it.

"That's pure wool, Tommy. One hundred percent."

"You can tell."

He took his arm back. "I want you to always remember me in this shirt."

I promised.

"And *winking* at you, like this," he said, giving me a manly, crow's-footed wink.

I promised I would always remember him in that shirt, winking at me exactly like that.

"And maybe *saying* something, something like . . . let's see . . ."

"'If only I bought those shares in Kodak.'"

He looked at me.

"I'm sorry," I said. "I just . . . I was just . . . I'm sorry."

He leaned closer. "I'm gonna tell you something, Tommy. Little secret. I never liked you very much. I always thought you were kind of a smart-ass."

"Yeah, well," I said, hitting back, "I always thought *you* were kind of a sonofabitch, Uncle Doug."

He laughed like hell. He liked that. "In this shirt," he said, holding out his sleeve again. "Feel that material."

"I just did."

"*Feel it again, dammit.*"

I felt it again. "Yeah," I said, humoring him, "they don't make shirts like this anymore."

He sprang to his feet. "They don't make *men* like this anymore," he said, poking himself in the chest. "Y'know that?"

I glanced at my alarm clock. "Uncle Doug," I said carefully, "I don't mean to be rude, okay? But it's after three in the morning. I have to get up in a few hours. So . . ."

He nodded, and sighed, and sat down again, heavily. "Must be nice," he said.

"What's that."

"Being alive. Must be awful nice."

"Not all *that* nice—getting up at six thirty in the morning to go to work with hardly any sleep, for example," I said to him, hinting.

But he wasn't listening. He was thinking about something. Then he looked at me with this wild sorrow on his face. "I blew it," he said. "Do you know that? I blew it, Tommy."

"Kodak, you mean?"

"Not Kodak, I'm not talking about Kodak, I'm talking about . . ." He stared off hard, looking for what he was talking about. Then his face softened. "I remember," he said quietly. "I was about your age, working construction. It was lunch break. I was sitting by myself on a girder at the top, twenty stories up. A nice day out, big blue sky, the city laid out below, me in the middle, eating a ham sandwich, with a thermos of coffee. The sandwich had a lot of mustard on it, Tommy, the way I always liked it. I sat there swinging my legs . . . eating that sandwich . . ."

I waited for more but there wasn't any. "Huh," I said.

He put his hands on his knees and pushed himself to his feet. "Remember me, Tommy."

"I will, Uncle Doug."

"In this shirt."

"I won't forget."

He stood there for a moment looking around. Then he gave me a manly wink, and was gone.

186,000 Miles per Second

---·◦·❮∞❯·◦·---

"Oh, Stan, it's ungodly big!"

"*Is* it? *Is* it?"

"A monstrosity!"

"*Is* it?"

"A pulsating radio star!"

"A what?"

"Don't stop!"

He didn't get that last bit but generally Stan loved the things Claire came out with during sex, especially concerning the size of his member, which in fact was only average but they enjoyed pretending otherwise. For a while Claire was calling it a phallus. "Oh, Stan," she would cry, "what a magnificent phallus!" That was when she was taking a night class in Greek mythology at the nearby community college. She told him he was hung like a centaur.

Claire was always taking a night class, not for a degree but because she was interested. Stan admired that about her, how smart she was and how interested in things like Greek mythology, or art history, or even something like geology. She took a geology class last year and that was all she talked about for a while, rocks. "Enough about the rocks, Claire, will ya?" he finally told her one night, then apologized and asked her to tell him more about the rocks, begged her to, and she eventually gave in.

After sex tonight, lying there relaxed, Stan asked her what she meant when she called his penis a pulsating radio star.

"I said that?"

"What the hell is a pulsating radio star?"

"A rotating neutron star that gives off a beam of electromagnetic radiation—called 'pulsars' for short," Claire answered, from the astronomy class she was currently taking.

Stan asked her what that had to do with his dick.

"The first pulsar was discovered in 1967," Claire continued, "approximately twenty-three thousand light years away, if I remember correctly." She paused. "You don't know about light years, do you, Stan."

He said he had to be honest.

She told him a light year represents the distance light travels in a year.

"Light travels?"

"Oh it travels, Stan. It travels."

"Never knew that."

"Care to know how fast?"

"Let's hear."

"One hundred and eighty-six thousand miles—ready for this?—per *second*."

"Jesus," he said, impressed.

"In one second it can travel seven times around the Earth. Seven times, Stan, in one second."

"That's bookin'," he agreed.

"So just think," she said, pointing at him, "just think how far it can travel in one *year.*"

"Pretty damn far, *I'd* say. Listen, I'm gonna get a drink of water. You want one?"

"No," she sighed. "Go ahead. Get your water."

Claire didn't like interruptions, so he was quick about it. And coming back he said to her right away, "Seven times around the Earth in one second—that's hard to believe."

"You think I'm making it up?"

"Of course not," he said, climbing in beside her. "I'm just saying it's hard to *imagine.*"

"Yeah?" she said. "Well imagine *this.* Imagine how—"

"Hey Claire?"

"What."

"Don't point at me like that, okay?"

"I'm trying to teach you something here, Stan."

"I know you are and I appreciate it. I just don't like being pointed at. You do it a lot. It's kind of annoying."

"I see," she said. "Well. I'm sorry. I won't point. In fact, why don't we talk about something else. How was your water?"

"Don't get like this."

"Like what, Stan?" she asked him, blinking.

"I want to hear about the traveling light, I really do. I just don't like when you stick your finger in my face, that's all. So go ahead. What was the speed of light again? I'm trying to remember."

She sighed, recited: "One hundred and eighty-six thousand miles per second."

"See now, that is amazing to me. I mean, how can anything travel that—?"

"Oh, stop. You're not interested."

"What're you talking about? I'm *very* interested. Come on, tell me some more."

She sat up a little. "All right," she said, nodding. "Fine. Let's talk about distances, shall we?"

"Bring it on."

"Do you have any idea, Stan, any idea at all how *far away* the stars are? Take a guess. Go ahead."

"Well, I would say . . . approximately speaking . . . millions and millions of miles. Or so."

She smiled at him sadly. "Okay. Listen up."

"I was way off, wasn't I."

"Stan, let me tell you something. There are stars out there—stars we can *see*—that are so far away they're not even *there* anymore."

"Explain," he said.

"Okay, it takes their light—which, remember, is traveling at 186,000 miles per second—"

"I remember."

"Going that fast, it still takes their light so long to get here? By the time it arrives, the star's been dead and gone a thousand years—in some cases millions. We're actually seeing something that hasn't been there for millions of years. So just *think*, Stan, how far away that has to be. Can you even begin to possibly imagine the kind of *distances* we're talking about here?"

He didn't say anything.

"Stan?"

"See, I don't like that."

She laughed. "What do you mean you don't *like* it?"

"Something being that far away."

"Stan, these are facts. These are scientific facts I'm giving you here."

"I don't care. I don't like it."

She touched his leg. "And remember: those are just the stars we're able to see. There are stars out there so far away, so *inconceivably—*"

"Drop it, Claire, will ya?"

She drew back and cocked her head. "What's the matter, Stan?"

"Nothing. I just think we've talked enough about the stars. It's after eleven and we should be getting to sleep now."

She nodded, slowly. "Interesting."

"Aw, don't start."

"Start what, Stan?" she asked him, blinking.

"Psychologizing me."

Claire took an introduction to psychology class last summer and they had some trouble for a while the way she kept analyzing everything he did, telling him the *real* reason he was doing it.

"I'm just curious," she said to him now. "You seem upset and I'm wondering—"

"I'm not upset. I'm tired, that's all." He reached for the lamp. "There's a difference." He switched it off.

"This is called 'avoidance coping,'" she told him in the dark.

He found her mouth and kissed it. "Goodnight, Claire."

"It's maladaptive, Stan," she added, turning on her side, away from him.

He scooted close and spread his hand on her stomach.

They lay there.

After a minute she asked him, "Can I tell you one more thing?"

"Is it about the universe?"

"Then I'll stop."

"Go ahead," he told her.

"It's expanding, Stan."

"Oh?" He brought his hand up to her breast and softly cupped it.

"Are you listening?"

"I'm right here."

"That's not what I asked."

"I'm listening."

"It's getting bigger, Stan."

He agreed, gently pressing himself against her.

"I'm talking about *space*," she said, and turned around to face him in the dark. "I'm talking about the distance *between* things—do you understand? What I'm trying to say? It's expanding, Stan. Every day it's getting—"

"Claire, are you pointing at me?"

"Ah, fuck it." She flipped over, facing the other way again.

He sighed and turned onto his back. He dropped his arm across his forehead.

They lay there like that.

After a little while Claire began softly snoring.

Staring up at the dark, Stan pictured them there: in their bed, in their room, in their house, in their town, their country, their planet, the camera receding at 186,000 miles per second, the Earth the size of a basketball, then a softball, then a baseball, then a golf ball, then gone, swallowed up in the dark that just went on and on—endlessly, pointlessly—on and on and *on*.

"Claire," he whispered, horrified.

THE WITCH OF
WITCH'S WOODS

After the lady opera singer was finally finished Ed
Sullivan said he had a bunch of acrobats from China
for us next and they all came running and tumbling out
and started doing acrobatic stuff with a lot of energy.

Karen goes, "*Must* they continually *smile* like that?"

She was on the other end of the couch. She's fifteen,
I'm twelve. I don't know why but lately she tries to
talk like the Queen of England.

I agreed, though, about the way these acrobats kept
smiling. It was boring. Their whole act was. They
were really good, I'm not saying they weren't, but it
was like watching a machine. I think they probably
practiced too much, you know? I actually think if they
started flying around the stage with smoke coming
out of their butts it would still be boring, just something they worked on every day for years. Now, if a
bunch of Chinese guys just came *along* and started
doing what they were doing, somersaulting onto each

other's shoulders and so on, that would be different, that would be something.

Know what I mean?

Afterwards Ed Sullivan came back again and said Señor Wences was next and I thought *Oh no*. He's on a lot. He's this old ventriloquist with an accent, Spanish I think, in a tuxedo, who talks to the side of his hand with a little wig on it and two eyes and lipstick like a mouth, moving the thumb up and down for a lower lip. He sets the hand on top of a headless little doll-boy's body, but there's no neck, which looks weird, the way the head is sunk between the shoulders like that. He calls the little boy Johnny. What gets me is the voice, Johnny's little voice, something about it.

"I'm turning this off," I told Karen, and got up.

"Please do, William."

She calls me William lately instead of Bill. I don't mind.

I slapped the off button and came back. "Can't handle that guy."

"The entire act is utterly creepy," she agreed.

"I hate when he has the hand give him a kiss."

"The man is clearly ill."

She went back to the book she was reading for school and I went back to my Sergeant Rock comic. Our mom was on a date with her latest boyfriend, this tall, nervous guy Mr. Mackenzie with an Adam's apple like Barney Fife. I read a couple pages of Sergeant Rock but kept thinking about Señor Wences, about Johnny, about his voice, this high, whispery, bashful voice with a Spanish accent. I don't know why but it gets to me, in the heart I mean. That's why I turned it off, because of the way Johnny gets to me with that little voice of his.

Karen asked me what I thought of Mom's new boyfriend.

I told her I didn't know. "What do *you* think?"

"He has extremely clammy hands."

"How do you know *that*?"

She acted it out: "'Karen? This is Mr. Mackenzie.'" She put out her hand, like to shake hands. "'How do you do, sir? It's very nice to . . . meet you.'" She took her hand back, slow, and wiped it on her T-shirt.

That was funny and I laughed and told her to do it again.

She wouldn't, though.

"Come on."

"It won't be nearly as humorous."

"Please?"

She did it again. She was right, it wasn't as funny.

We went back to reading. I like Sergeant Rock, the way he wears his helmet tilted back with the straps hanging loose and the way he's tough with his men but only because he cares about them.

Karen gave a big sigh. "I despise this book."

"What is it?"

"A play, for English. A group of young girls accuse various people in the village of being witches and they hang them."

"The girls?"

"The witches. Except, supposedly they weren't."

"Witches?"

"According to the author, the girls were all lying."

"So this really happened?"

"In Salem, Massachusetts, in the year . . . hold on."

I asked Karen if she thought there really are witches.

"Sixteen ninety-two. Of *course* there are."

I asked her if she thought there was a witch living in Witch's Woods. That's the woods about a mile from here.

"Why do you suppose it's *called* Witch's Woods, William?"

"Because there's really a *witch* in there?"

"Obviously."

I wanted to hear about this. "What does she . . . how does she . . . I mean, is she . . . ? *Tell* me about her."

"You've never heard the story?"

"Tell me."

Karen put the book in her lap and folded her hands over it. "All right. This was many years ago."

"Like *sixteen*-something?"

"No, more like forty years ago. There was a wedding."

"At Saint Bart's?" That's our church, Saint Bartholomew's.

"I'm not certain. But the reception was held at the KC hall. You know where *that* is, I presume."

"Near the woods."

"Exactly. So. Anyway. These three drunks at the reception, these three intoxicated males, these three cretins—"

"What's that mean?"

"Morons. These three cretinous morons talked one of the bridesmaids into accompanying them on a little walk into the woods, saying they wanted to show her something, some exotic flowers that grew there."

"And she believed them?"

"She was apparently quite intoxicated herself."

"Maybe they slipped something into her drink. I saw this movie the other night—"

"Do you mind?"

I told her go ahead.

"So they took her into the woods," she said, then tried to use this spooky voice on me: "*Took her deep, deep into the woods, where it was very, very—*"

"Don't do the voice."

"Too frightening?"

"Too dumb."

She went on in her regular voice. "So anyway they tied her to a tree and left her there."

"Where'd they get the rope?"

"I have no idea."

"They left her there overnight?"

"She was found the next morning, still alive, but her hair . . . was completely . . ."

"Gone," I said.

She got mad. "Don't *do* that, will you? When I pause like that, don't jump in with something, just wait."

"Sorry." I wanted to hear this. "Her hair . . . ?" I said, and waited.

"Had turned completely . . ."

I waited.

"White," she said.

"From fear?" I said.

"Obviously."

I asked her what she saw, what was out there that made her hair turn white.

"I don't know. Perhaps nothing. But *you* try spending an entire night in the pitch-dark woods tied to a tree, see how *you* look in the morning."

"So . . . now she *lives* out there?"

"In that old shed. You can just see it from the path."

I didn't understand. "Why would she want to live out there if it scared her so much?"

"To be away from the world," she said. "Away from people. Away from men."

I asked Karen if she'd ever seen her out there.

She nodded at me, slow.

"No, really?"

"Yes, really."

"What did she look like?"

She shrugged. "A crone."

"A crow?"

"A *crone*."

"What's that?"

"A dried-up, wrinkled old woman."

"What was she wearing?"

"A salmon-colored taffeta dress with a velveteen bolero jacket and matching heels," she said, just like that.

Then it hit me and I pointed at her. "From the *wedding*."

Karen gave another slow nod.

That was creepy and sad about the dress. "Must be pretty raggedy by now," I said.

"Somewhat."

I wanted to know more. "So how does she get by? What does she eat?"

"Mushrooms, bugs, and such."

"What about, you know, going to the bathroom?" I asked, because there wouldn't be a toilet in that little shed.

"She has the entire woods," Karen pointed out.

I didn't like the picture in my head of this old woman squatting down, in that dress. "Does she ever wash herself?"

"William . . ."

"What."

"The woman . . . is a witch."

"They don't wash?"

"Are you being facetious?"

"What does that mean?"

"It means are you joking?"

I wasn't. And what made her a witch anyway? Just because she didn't wash? I asked her about that.

I had it backwards, Karen told me. "She's not a witch because she doesn't wash, she doesn't wash because she's a witch."

"Okay, but what makes her a witch instead of just this scary-looking, smelly old lady?"

Karen explained, like a very patient teacher. "After someone has been alone like that, completely and utterly alone for a long, long time, especially if she happens to be a woman, she begins to develop certain . . . shall we say . . . *powers*."

I sat up. "Powers, what do you mean powers, what're you talking about? Explain."

"I *mean*," she said, "she has acquired certain magical skills, especially in the casting of spells."

"She can cast spells?"

"That is correct."

"What kind?"

"Apparently she's very good at transformations."

"How do you mean?"

"The turning of things into other things."

"Turning what things? Into what?"

"Turning boys, for example."

"Into what."

"Into girls."

"Get out."

Karen leaned forward. "That's her revenge, do you see? On males. On the entire gender."

"You're making this up."

She sat back. "Of course." She took up her book again. "Of course I am," she said, looking for her place.

I went back to my comic book, to Sergeant Rock and the combat-happy joes of Easy Company. But I couldn't concentrate. I tried but I couldn't. "So," I said, "do you *know* anyone? Who got . . . you know . . ."

She looked at me over her book. "Changed? Do I know anyone who got changed?"

"Do you?" I was feeling clammier than Mom's Mr. Mackenzie by now.

Karen put her book down again. "I wasn't ever going to tell you this, but perhaps I should. Perhaps this is something you should know."

"Is it scary? Another scary thing?" I wasn't sure I had room.

"Do you recall when I told you I had seen her?"

"The witch?"

"Do you recall?"

It was only a couple of minutes ago. I said, "Yeah . . . ?"

"Well, that was true. It was several years ago. You were a mere toddler. I *did* see her, but what I failed to mention, what I *didn't* say . . ."

I waited.

"When I saw her . . ."

I waited.

"I was a little boy, William."

"Quit it."

"I was your older *brother*."

"Quit it, Karen. That's not even funny."

"No," she said, "you're right." Then she looked off. "It's not," she said. Then her face crumpled up. She looked down at her lap and started crying.

With Karen though, you can never be sure. I leaned down trying to see her face. "Are you really crying?"

She kept on. She was really crying. I didn't know what to do. I got up and went over. I put my hand on her shoulder.

"I'm still a *boy*," she said. "It's not . . . my . . . *fault*," she said, and started crying even harder.

I wasn't exactly sure what she was talking about but I patted her shoulder and said, "I know . . . I know . . ."

She looked at me, her face all red and wet and puffed up and ugly. "You don't even know what I'm talking about, so don't say you know, because you don't. Nobody does." She looked down and went back to crying. "*Nobody*," she said.

But then all of a sudden I kind of *did* know, and it popped out, "But I *do* know, Karen."

She stopped crying on a dime and looked at me. "What do you know?"

I shrugged.

"Tell me."

"I have to use the bathroom."

"*Tell* me, William."

So I told her: "You have a crush on Cynthia Kellogg."

She stared at me, bug-eyed. Then she said, real quiet, "You looked in my journal." Her diary, she meant. "Didn't you," she said.

I looked down at my feet, meaning yes.

"Oh . . . my . . . *God*," she said.

It has a lock on it but also a tiny key at the end of a string. Mostly she writes about school, how she hates this, hates that, sometimes about our mom, the way she gets about every new boyfriend, how pathetic it is. Not much about me. She did mention me having my tonsils out last summer, just mentioned it. But there's also, every now and then, a little report about Cynthia Kellogg, what she was wearing today, how pretty she looked in it, what a bonehead Cynthia's boyfriend Gary was, sometimes whole pages about what a gigantic crush Karen has on her. She used the word "crush," so that's why *I* did.

She was sitting there covering her face with her hands telling me to go away, to please go away right now and leave her alone.

But I didn't want to. I didn't want to leave her like that, feeling like that, all ashamed like that. I still had my hand on her shoulder and I kept it there and told her it was no big deal. I told her about Johnny, the way I felt about Johnny, that little hand with lipstick, on Ed Sullivan, the little Spanish boy with the bashful voice. I told Karen I had a crush on him, which wasn't exactly true, I wouldn't call it a crush exactly, but maybe it was, maybe that was the right word, I don't know.

She took her hands away from her face and looked at me. "Wait," she said. "You're saying . . . you have a crush . . . on that's guy's *hand?*"

"I like the little voice," I said. "The way he speaks."

With just her finger and thumb she took my hand off her shoulder, kind of slow and careful, like she didn't want to hurt my feelings, *but.* "That's pretty bizarre, William. Pretty peculiar, wouldn't you say?"

I gave a shrug, meaning what can you do?

"I'm sorry," she said, "but that's . . ." She gave a laugh. "That's pretty weird."

I laughed too. Why not? It *was* pretty weird. Anyway, Karen didn't feel so much like she had to be ashamed about having a crush on Cynthia Kellogg, not with *me* anyway, with someone who's got a crush on a puppet, and not even an *actual* puppet, just some old guy's painted-up *hand.*

I went back to my side of the couch, Karen telling me if I ever looked in her journal again she would personally scoop out both of my eyes with a teaspoon. "I mean that sincerely."

I told her, "Okay."

She went back to her book.

But I still had some questions. All that stuff about the witch—how much of it was true? Any of it? *Was* there even a witch out there? I asked her.

She gave me the line she started with: If there *wasn't* one, why would they call the place Witch's Woods?

"That's it?" I said. "That's all you've got?"

"Sorry."

"So you never actually really saw her?"

"Not literally."

"What does *that* mean?"

"Means no."

I sat back. I didn't like hearing that. I didn't want it to be *all* made up. I liked the idea of a witch out there. I wouldn't want to go visit her, I wouldn't want anything to do with her. But I liked having her out there. I wanted stuff like witches to be real. Otherwise, what have we got? Chinese acrobats.

You know?